PROFESSOR BERNICE SUMMERFIELD
AND THE GLASS PRISON

Jacqueline Rayner

BIG FINISH

Also available in this series:

Professor Bernice Summerfield and the Dead Men Diaries
ISBN 1-903654-00-9

Professor Bernice Summerfield and the Doomsday Manuscript
ISBN 1-903654-04-1

Professor Bernice Summerfield and the Gods
of the Underworld
ISBN 1-903654-23-8

Professor Bernice Summerfield and the Squire's Crystal
ISBN 1-903654-13-0

Professor Bernice Summerfield and the Infernal Nexus
ISBN 1-903654-16-5

Published by Big Finish Productions Ltd,
PO Box 1127
Maidenhead SL6 3LW

www.bernicesummerfield.com

Range editor: Gary Russell
Managing Editor: Jason Haigh-Ellery

First published December 2001

Professor Bernice Summerfield and the Glass Prison
© Jacqueline Rayner 2001

The moral right of the author has been asserted

Bernice Summerfield was created by Paul Cornell
Irving Braxiatel was created by Justin Richards
Jason Kane was created by Dave Stone

ISBN 1–903654–41–6

Cover art by Adrian Salmon © 2001
Design by Clayton Hickman
Logo designed by Paul Vyse

Printed and bound in Great Britain by Biddles Ltd
www.biddles.co.uk

For my godmother, Rosalind Chesney, with love

1
Just Another Brick
in the Wall

On a clear day, I can see for miles.

That's because all the walls are made of glass. All except the walls I've built around myself, because I need strong walls that no one can breach. Because I don't want to be hurt any more. And I need to be protected – I think.

You see, I'm having a baby.

The only problem is, I don't know if it's mine.

Even they seem to draw the line at hurting a pregnant woman. Well, when I say hurting, I mean deliberately torturing. They did that to some of the others – I know they did it to Claire and Gripper when we came in, because I had to watch. You see everything in here. There's nothing you can do about it, unless you close your eyes.

They were surrounding us when we staggered out from the crash. I was a bit dazed at the time, and for a few moments thought they were just jolly officials concerned for our health. Wrong! The red-and-silver Fifth Axis uniforms were a bit of a giveaway, once the smoke cleared and I was able to do thinking once again, e.g. remember my name and where I was. The first of the answers I was reasonably happy with – Professor Bernice Surprise Summerfield, which, all things considered, is a fairly good name; I can certainly think of a lot worse. For example, I know a girl called Chlamydia. But as for where I was...

'Civilians!' I choked. 'Accidental civilians! That is, here accidentally. We're quite deliberately civilians. I'm Professor Summerfield, and this is –' I looked around for Claire, but I couldn't see her. There was a split second of panic as I almost dived back into the burning wreck, and then I remembered that Claire is, of course, over two feet shorter then me, so I angled my gaze downwards and looked around again. There she was, chumbling towards me, bits of scorched shuttle sticking haphazard here and there on her ginger fur.

'Benny!' she was squeaking. 'Benny, are you all right?'

I assured her I was, and gave her a big relieved hug. Which didn't go down too well with our new associates. 'No contact! Hands in the air!'

I half-raised my hands unenthusiastically. Okay, so theoretically I should be amazed to still be alive, what with having just transgressed hostile airspace and all, but over the years still being alive has happened to me almost constantly and if I were to be surprised about it whenever something like this happens my eyes and mouth would be in permanent cartoon 'O's. Instead I do a general thanks to the Goddess every week and just get on with things, and I'm damned if I'm going to be gracious to some jumped-up military type just because he's done me the favour of not having my craft shot down and me killed. So far.

'Hands up! Right up! Now!' He was waving a gun just below my eyebrows.

Sometimes discretion is the better part of valour, and it never hurts anyone to be gracious, even to jumped-up military types. I raised my hands right up now. Beside me, Claire was waving her little hamster paws just as high as they would go.

They searched us, confiscated everything but the clothes we stood up in, and marched us into the back of a truck. There were just the two of us for the journey to the Glass Prison – not that we knew where we were going at the time, obviously. Claire started crying – in typical Claire fashion she was crying more for me than herself. It's weird, but somehow I wasn't able to take the situation seriously. I've been in so many similar situations so many times. I reassured Claire, told her that we were neutral civilians and not subject to Fifth Axis law; we'd explain how the shuttle had developed a fault and we hadn't intentionally invaded their

2

airspace, and even if the worst came to the worst and they didn't believe us, Irving Braxiatel would find a way to get us out somehow. Even if he didn't... know... where... we... were... going. Damn, damn, damn.

Anyway, even the Fifth Axis would treat a heavily-pregnant woman (and I do mean *heavily*) with some respect, wouldn't they? I even made a joke of it, telling her that if we'd stayed on the Braxiatel Collection I'd shortly have murdered both my ex-husband Jason Kane and father of the child Adrian Wall, and then I'd be being put in prison for real and then where would we be?!

For real. Like somehow this wasn't real, that it was all a big joke.

Laughing in the face of adversity, that's me.

If I'd known there was this much adversity coming up, I'd have died laughing.

Even before I'd seen *him*.

They say that after birth you can stimulate the baby to relax by playing it sounds that it associates with its mother being calm. I have, therefore, been practising being calm while simultaneously shouting and throwing crockery. In this way I am guaranteed a permanently relaxed baby.

Whether I'll still have anyone to shout at by the time this baby is born is another matter altogether.

'The way of the Killoran is to embrace the pain of childbirth, as a sacrifice to the creators in thanks for the gift of life.'

Well, I'm not a Killoran. And although I feel that in many ways I should be in favour of wholly natural childbirth, I've suffered so much unavoidable *pain in my life that I believe I'm justified in deciding not to embrace* avoidable *pain now I have the option.*

Brax wants to hire in a midwife; he thinks I'm overdoing it. I've pointed out to him that I'm perfectly capable of looking after myself, thank you very much, without some bossy do-gooder trying to make me feel guilty every time I try to lift so much as a teacup.

3

He says that unless I agree he's going to ask Ms Jones (who happens to be our resident first-aider) to supervise the birth. 'Push! Push now, I tell you! Right, that's it, if you don't get that baby out right now I shall be forced to suspend your library privileges!'

Okay, maybe I'll think about getting a midwife...

Jason... well, I'm not sure if Jason's really talking to me. I don't think Jason's really sure if he's talking to me.

'I don't know why you expect me to care. It's not my baby.'

'Well, of course it isn't! We've been divorced for years and anyway I thought you were dead!'

'So that makes it all right to bear another man's child, does it?'

'Well... yes! Yes, of course it does! And you know damn well it didn't happen like that, anyway.'

'Like what?'

'Like... like through my own choice. I'm carrying something inside me that I don't know anything about. I didn't choose it, it chose me.'

'Yeah, yeah, heard it all before.'

'And you're going to hear it again and again until you get into your thick (but incidentally getting slightly thin on top) head exactly what it means.'

'Oh, I understand all right. I just don't care. I'm going out now. And I have a full head of hair, thank you very much.'

'I'm not waiting up for you!'

'Oooh, I'm so upset. Still, try not to snore as loudly as usual – you might disturb the baby.'

'Get out of this room now!'

'Gladly. Anyway, I happen to have a date.'

'A date! You're bringing back tarts and telling them you'll get them into the movies!'

Door slams.

Plate hits door just as it shuts; shatters loudly.

Benny starts to cry.

It must be my hormones.

* * *

4

I'd heard of the Glass Prison on Deirbhile – Deirbhile being a tiny planet with a single landmass, but a great strategic position. The prison is one of those buildings, like the Taj Mahal or the tomb of Mausolus or the Pyramids of Mars, that everyone knows about. Not that it's been shortlisted as a wonder of the universe – or not yet, anyway. But, also like the Taj Mahal etc., it's a beautiful building with a dark heart. Have you heard the story of the Taj Mahal? It's from Earth; India. This sultan's wife died, and he wanted to build the most incredible monument to house her tomb, show how much he cared. So he gets his architects to come up with this superb building. They surpass themselves, and build the most fantastic place ever. Everyone marvels at it. And then what does he do? He cuts off the hands of all the craftsmen who built it, so they can never make anything to rival it.

That story really tells you everything about humans you'll ever need to know.

Actually, the tale goes on that the Sultan intended to build a mirroring tomb for himself, one of black marble to compliment the white Taj Mahal. One can only imagine the forehead-slapping that must have gone on when he realised there weren't any handy craftsmen left to do it.

History is littered with tales of humans building wonderful things through death and horror. There are all the slaves who died to make the pyramids – not to mention all the poor people put to death so some undeserving pharaoh would have faithful servants in the afterlife. I wonder if the odd pharaoh got an unpleasant surprise upon entering the land of the dead and finding they had to spend eternity with a load of rather pissed-off Egyptians. After all, he could hardly threaten to put them to death if they didn't do what he said...

And woe betide anyone who's told 'we'd like you to build a fiendish maze. Lots of puzzles, unavoidable traps, that sort of thing. Oh, and we don't want anyone to know how it was done. You can keep a secret, can't you?' Rumour has it that the people who installed the security systems in the Glass

Prison met with 'little accidents' some time later. But that might just be a rumour.

Taking those examples of how humans behave, maybe you can even understand the general thinking behind the Glass Prison. It's almost as close as you can get to the perfect gaol – talking relatively, here, from the imprisoner's point of view and assuming they're not interested in things like justice or rehabilitation or human rights (and believe me, if the Fifth Axis were handed a human rights treaty you'd be lucky if it even deigned to wipe its ugly fascist bottom on it). Of course, the *really* perfect gaol would be where you chucked everyone into a big pit with six-foot-thick reinforced concrete walls and threw away the key. But the Axis is too organised for that. Has to have things a bit more formal. Has to pretend it's civilised. Has to make sure it can still get information from you. Has to make sure that you're observed all the time.

All the time... OH GODDESS, THEY WATCH US *ALL THE TIME*!

Calm, calm, calm. Take a deep breath.

The Glass Prison. Description of. It's like a twenty-first century office block crossed with a fairy-tale castle. If you could see it from a distance, you really would think it beautiful. In fact, you can even get holo-postcards of it. That possibly tells you something else about humans. That they think a place of tremendous human suffering suitable for recreational exploitation. I wonder how many tourists (in the days before the exclusion zone) sent off cheerful little pictures of this nightmare inscribed 'wish you were here'.

All I could think when we were approaching it was, 'it's so big!' On a postcard, it's only three and a half inches high. In real life it's a greenhouse the size of a hill. And the scariest thing of all was the people. Inside, looking out. Eleven storeys of despairing beings, living their lives, staring out to the freedom they could all but touch.

They weren't shown on the postcards. And I was about to become one of them.

6

The prison isn't actually made of glass, of course, that wouldn't be much good for security; it just looks like it I don't know what the stuff is, except it's pretty good at soundproofing, and so far I've not been able to scratch it. Not that I've anything to scratch it with, apart from my fingernails.

There was one benefit to the soundproofing, though. You know I mentioned earlier how they tortured Claire? Well, at least I couldn't hear the screams.

I don't want to think any more about that time.

Tell you what, I'll explain about Claire.

Claire is my midwife. Brax finally got his way, so he and I interviewed about thirty people for the post – he said I was too hard on the candidates, but what I say is, if a person's going to be responsible for bringing a child into the world, they really ought to be able to have their own ideas on the significance of ziggurats, know a lot of good chocolate recipes, and at least give me a good run for my money at Scrabble. Anyway, it didn't matter how many of them walked out, because the moment I saw Claire I knew she was going to look after me. I'd had a good feeling about her even before the interview – a sort of sad good feeling, and a very illogical one, but you see my mother was called Claire, and I can't seem to get my head round the idea that someone could bear the name and not be a good person. And then I met Claire herself and she snuffled her nose just like one of my closest friends, Keri, does, and we were friends straight away, bless her furry little Pakhar cheeks. And then it turned out she'd read my book (*Down Among the Dead Men*, available from all good bookstores) and could make a phenomenal chocolate cheesecake. She also actually managed to beat me at Scrabble, but it was mainly luck. Oh, all right, she did get 'quincunx' on a triple word score, which shows not only skill but also an excellent vocabulary. I eventually forgave her, though.

Claire's been wonderful since the beginning. Sometimes she fussed, but I coped. And she coped with me, which was the most amazing thing of all. Coped with me and the baby and our hideously complicated story.

I suppose I should tell that tale, too, while I'm on a nostalgia kick for the time in my life when I wasn't in prison. I almost can't remember it now.

Once upon a time, I became… detached from my body, which was then taken over by a centuries-old sorceress, who, incidentally, is currently living in a hole under the ground of the asteroid where I live, and has the guise of a man in his mid-forties. While I was 'absent', my body was impregnated by a seven-foot-tall Killoran called Adrian Wall, who is now in love with me – but who also hates my guts. If you think you're confused, imagine how he feels.

Eventually I got my body back, and I was a bit freaked out by it all. I confess that I did feel violated – still do – but I know that Adrian believed me to be… well, me, and happy about the whole thing, and in my heart of hearts I don't condemn him for it. My baby was conceived through passion, not hatred, and that makes it easier. Easier, but not, of course, easy.

So, we know Adrian's the father – even though I toyed for a while with the idea of trying to persuade my ex-husband Jason, recently rescued by me from a demon dimension, that it was his instead. Jason and I had wanted children, once. I think – I *know* – that part of the reason we split up, in the end, was because it just wasn't happening. And not for want of trying. In some alternative future, some other universe, we were happy parents, but I knew almost as soon as I thought about it that I couldn't pretend. Couldn't go through with it. Not fair. The baby's Adrian's, whether I like that or not. But we don't know who the mother is. Is it me, biological mum, whose tubes and holes and spongy bits were used – or ancient evil sorceress Avril, who was mental mum at conception time? (Ugh ugh ugh ugh ugh – still don't like to think about that.) And apart from all the psychological issues, there're the purely practical ones too – like we can't find anything on record about a human/Killoran crossbreed, and we don't even know stuff like how long the gestation period is likely to be. Nine Earth-standard months as for a human, or shorter as for a Killoran? Will it have hair or fur? Will it be born with its eyes closed or open?

Sometimes I'm convinced that what I'm carrying inside me is half dog-man, half witch, and nothing to do with me at all, and I want to claw it out. That's one of the reasons Brax wanted me to have a live-in midwife, to stop me doing that. To stop me feeling that. And yes, Claire has helped. She calms me down. She tells me it's mine. She tells me I'm growing it, nurturing it, and it'll be part of me whatever. I can't quite believe her, though. And when I'm really down I tell myself I'm glad it's not mine. Because then I won't cry so much when I lose it.

'Now, we're going to practice breathing techniques. Benny, breath in like this...'

'Hang on, shouldn't she be lying down?'

'I think you'll find that this is the correct procedure. Have you ever had a baby, Mr Kane?'

'Yeah, I've had triplets. Look, I've had more real world experience than you have, mate...'

'Really? I doubt that very much.'

'This breathing lark is pointless. Yer just supposed to lie there and the whelp slides out. That's the Killoran way of things.'

'Could you three please be quiet? Benny is trying to –'

'SHUT UP! Will everyone just SHUT UP! This is my body; it's nothing to do with ANY OF YOU!'

'Benny, where are you going? Benny, come back, please! This is important!'

DAY –7, MORNING

When I woke up this morning, Gripper was sitting on the edge of my bunk, staring at me. 'Aaaargh!' I yelled, surprised, and then tried to pretend I'd just stubbed my toe on the corner post. I will show no fear! I really wish she wouldn't do that. Gripper was a Fifth Axis assassin. She doesn't seem to mind people knowing. I'd have thought that it'd be the sort of thing you kept to yourself, because people in a Fifth Axis gaol aren't likely to have fluffy-bunny feelings for members of the elite. Turns out I'm wrong. Because the Fifth Axis are such suspicious bastards that half the folks in here are ex-military, and no one wants to start an internal war. Plus the non-military types are generally too wary of people who had job titles like 'assassin' to take them on. Of course, there's always the cult. The cultists don't appear to be scared of anyone. But then, they have other things on their minds.

During the first week Claire and I took turns to stay up all night and keep an eye on Gripper, just in case, but eventually we got so stressed by lack of sleep that we gave it up. After all, as Gripper herself pointed out, if she were in fact a plant, in there to kill us, she'd have done it by now. It's not as if the guards would care.

She just likes freaking people out. And what's really annoying me is that it's working.

I'm not supposed to be that sort of person. I'm not meant to get freaked out so easily. I should be able to ignore it. Laugh at how pathetic she must be to get her kicks that way.

Gripper's full name is Agrippina. Named after this Roman chick who killed lots of people. I have a suspicion that Gripper adopted the name herself, and was probably born something unthreatening like 'Doris' or 'Petunia'. Actually, that was Sophia's theory – she's very into the importance of names – but one with which I agreed. But I'm getting ahead of myself. You haven't met Sophia yet. Anyway, Gripper: she's human, tall and blonde and ice-maideny. I really don't like her.

I kicked her off the bed, and splashed cold water on my face from the wash jug. Felt a bit better. Ran my fingers through my hair and tried to tidy it a bit – thank goodness I don't have long tresses like Gripper, because I haven't been able to earn enough credits yet to get myself a comb. The

Wolf won't let me do any work because of the baby – more on that later. I did try to talk to the guards about basic needs such as soap and toothpaste, but they don't give a damn because they're all Aseks. I'd never met an Asek before I came to the Glass Prison. You'd probably think they were androids, if you didn't know otherwise. They're humanoid, with completely smooth skin – no body hair, not even eyelashes – and they're utterly devoid of colour. Even their eyes are solid white. Their noseless faces look like eggs with two lightly-pencils circles halfway up and a small hole just below with which they occasionally talk. There are slight variations in body shape and possibly – I can't quite make my mind up – extremely slight differences in facial features, such as they are, but as none of the Aseks seem to have personalities they might as well be clones. Actually, I have a theory that they're not a natural race at all, but a product of Fifth Axis genetic engineering. 'Asek' is from 'asexual': they are not man, woman or hermaphrodite, and consequently have little feeling towards those of us who are. There's a girl called Edie on C floor, a prostitute who's been locked up before in normal places, and she keeps trying it on with them anyway. Can't seem to get it into her head that they are entirely indifferent to her. There's no one who'll smuggle out a message, or oblige by bringing in a sneaky bottle of shampoo or a lipstick in return for favours. I feel a bit sorry for her, really.

Claire squeaked to let me know she was awake and ready to get up. 'Come on, then, little legs,' I said, reaching up for her. She won't let me take her weight, so she sort of jumps and I sort of swing her on to the floor. I learned early on that Claire has to make things easy for me. For example, there are two double bunks in our cell. Gripper had already staked a claim to one of the lower bunks and wasn't shifting, and Claire insisted I had the other bottom one, even though she's only three feet tall and needs a stepladder to brush her teeth. I was perfectly happy to take the top one myself, but the thing is, Claire would then have been totally miserable worrying about me and the baby. I can't have the luxury of suffering any more, not now there's something else to worry about. Some*one* else. Mustn't keep thinking of it as a thing.

Of course, as events turned out, I thank the Goddess I've got the bottom bunk. At least some of the time I'm hidden from view. If he were able to watch me sleep... well, I don't think I'd ever sleep again.

'I can't take it any more, Claire. Sod the lot of them, I'm out of here.'

'But Benny, it's too risky, we don't know when the baby's due...'

'I'll find some planet with good hospital facilities. I'll be fine.'

'Don't, Benny, please! If something happened to you I'd never forgive myself.'

'Look, it's my responsibility. And that's the problem. I can't cope with five or six people thinking they have the right to tell me how to do things. Especially when they're all coming out with completely contradictory stuff anyway. Brax is being a know-it-all, as usual. Adrian's ideas of parenthood are not mine, to say the least. Jason... well, Jason seems to veer between jealousy and obsession. He spends days ignoring me – and he seems to have picked up some floozy to show he really doesn't care – and then he goes and barges in on me in the middle of the night to weep drunkenly at me and tell me that the baby should have been ours. I have to get away from it, for my own sanity. I've packed my rucksack, left Wolsey in charge of the automatic can-opener, and set the vid recorder for Buffy the Vampire Slayer *season 792. I'm leaving. '*

'Then I'm coming with you.'

'No, Claire, you don't have to...'

'Yes I do. I was hired to look after you, and I'm going to do that whatever. Just you try and stop me! But I wish you'd change your mind. Stay here...'

'No way. This is the last place in the universe I want to be. Nowhere could be worse than the Braxiatel Collection at the moment...'

I HATE BEING WATCHED!

You know, I was never a big fan of zoos. I can see the conservation aspect: preserve the porcupine, save the stegosaurus, care for the only breeding pair of sand beasts in the galaxy. But, you know, I wonder if the animals would rather be extinct than be observed twenty-four/seven (Earth-standard).

I HATE THIS!

Can you tell it's getting to me?

Being locked up. This I can cope with. I have had to do so many, many times. That's not to say I like it and wouldn't want to get out at the first opportunity, but if we're talking simple *coping*, living day to day, then I'm Bearing-It Girl. (As opposed to Baring-It Girl, ha ha, because I keep my smock on ALL THE TIME. Well, sort of. I have to admit to taking the odd private moment to glance down my top, because it's such a change to have something there to notice. This might seem ridiculous to you, but if you'd spent your whole adult life with just a touch of an inferiority complex about the size of a certain part of your anatomy, which then became an acceptable – nay, more than acceptable! – dimension for a limited period only... well, you'd want to keep peeking too.) Anyway. Looking at myself is one thing. Imagining admiring glances from others is another (I'm deliberately ignoring the bit of my body that looks like I've swallowed three watermelons whole). But more than that is a whole different ballgame altogether. Which brings me to my next point...

Being watched.

You don't usually get much privacy in gaol – surprise, surprise. BUT YOU GET NO PRIVACY AT ALL WHEN THE GAOL IS MADE OF GLASS!

Gripper always seems to be looking my way. I suppose it's force of habit with her; she needs someone to keep tabs on. I can cope with that by feeling superior. There are the cult women. They're always looking at me too. And I don't like that very much, but I avoid them during the day and there are a lot of others between my cell and theirs.

But then there's *him*.

I couldn't believe it when I first saw him. Just looked up and there he was. You switch off after it's over, don't you? Drink the champagne, slap each other on the back, maybe shed a few tears depending on the circumstances. Bad guys out of your life, hurrah, hurrah! Forget that they might carry on, have lives after you've foiled their dastardly plan. Obviously, had I thought about it particularly, I'd have realised that after I'd framed him as a traitor, Fifth Axis Kolonel Daglan Straklant – if he survived – would end up in an Axis traitors' prison. Of course, even if I *had* thought about it particularly, I'd have had to be having a particularly bad or excessively precognisant day to imagine I'd end up in a cell almost directly below him.

I'm not sure if it's a sign of civilised behaviour that the prison is split into male and female floors, or just because the Axis does and probably always will believe that men – even imprisoned men – are the superiors. There are more male than female prisoners – the men almost all ex-military, whereas a number of the women are obstructive natives or pros accused of sleeping with the enemy. Or civilians, like Claire and I, who were in the wrong place at the wrong time, and thought to be spies. The bottom floor, A floor, is admin, staff quarters, all that stuff. Where we were brought when we first arrived. Where the interrogation happens. Then you go up B, C and D, all female floors. I'm on D – cell D20 to be precise. There are 30 cells on D, each containing four prisoners (or supposed to, anyway). There's D1–8 along the far side, then a corridor in front of them, then a double block of D9–D16 and D17–D24 in the middle, another corridor, then D25–D30 at the front of the floor. The dining room is in the front right corner, where cells D31 and D32 would be if they existed. Another corridor surrounds the entire perimeter, and the single external door – always locked, except during open sessions or when Aseks change shifts – is in the corner near the dining room. There's no staff room,

14

nothing like that. The Aseks continually patrol while on duty. They don't socialise, even with each other. I wonder if they even socialise when off duty. Do they have feelings at all?

Above our floor, E floor upwards are men-only, all the way to K. The higher up you are the more sunlight you get, but the further you have to fall – if pushed. I've heard rumours that women who upset the system suddenly find they've 'accidentally wandered' on to the male section during an E–K open session. I don't think I need to spell it out any further. The rumours say they don't come back.

But incredibly, being on the 'border floor' (as it's called) is considered a huge bonus. In front of you, the corridor complete with Asek patrols, to each side and below, other all-female dorms, but on the sixth side – the ceiling... men. A lot of the girls make much cash out of it during open sessions, when all the lower floors are allowed to mingle, letting others use their dorms. I mean, I'm a pretty experienced woman of the world, but even I was slightly surprised just exactly what people can get up to with a solid sheet of soundproofed glass-substance between them. If my darling ex-hubby were here, he'd be able to collect material for a dozen of his borderline-illegal holovids.

I'm avoiding the subject of *him*. I notice I'm doing that a lot lately.

Thing is, when you've destroyed someone's life, it's a bit of a bummer to find out they're living a couple of yards away.

'Mmm... Claire, what time is it?'
  'Early. Sorry, did I wake you?'
  'I thought I heard voices. Were you on the comms link?'
  'No!'
  'Claire, I can tell when you're fibbing. Your fur blushes. Who were you calling?'
  'Mr Braxiatel. Sorry. I thought I'd better let him know you're all right.'
  'Claire! I told you I wanted them to stew for a bit!'
  'But... that's not really very nice, is it? Everyone will be

worrying about you.'

'Well, it serves them right. They should have appreciated me while they had me. I hope you didn't tell them our flight path. Don't want anyone coming after us.'

'No. No, I didn't do that.'

'Good.'

2
One Week to Go

Straklant looked different. Well, it had been about ten months since I'd seen him, and he'd probably been in here for most of that. Probably following some pretty horrendous interrogation. I'd have almost feel sorry for him, if he wasn't a mass-murdering git.

I'd first met Kolonel Daglan Straklant at Brax's New Year's Party. He broke Wolsey's paw in an effort to get to know me, and then pretended to be a good guy for a while so I'd help him track down a manuscript. He killed quite a few people along the way. In the end, Brax and I tricked him into giving us the security codes that allowed us to foil the Axis takeover of the planet Kasagrad. I'm guessing that his Axis colleagues weren't very happy when they found him again.

They must have taken his false hand away – the one concealing a poisoned spike – his left arm ended in a wrist stump. He'd been slim before, now he was skinny. His hair was still that stunning blond, but instead of the sharp military cut it straggled almost to his chin. He had a beard too, as did most of the male prisoners. No blades allowed, you see, and you had to save up a hell of a lot of credits to get a laser-razor. (It was a problem on female floors, too. If you lined up all the women and looked at the bits between hem and ankle, you'd think you were in a forest of hobbits.)

The one thing that hadn't changed a bit about Straklant was his cold, cold eyes. It was on the second morning that I saw him – I was in D19, the cell next door to ours, talking to a girl called Deedee who turned out to know someone who knew someone who might once have been a student at the university I used to teach at – anyway, I just glanced up and there he was. I knew him at once, of course. He was staring down at me. I've never, ever caught him unawares. Even if he's not looking directly at me, I can tell that he damn well knows I'm looking up and doesn't care at all. I've yo-yoed between avoiding him, ignoring him, and doing my best to embarrass him by making rude gestures or silly faces or doing the dozy chicken dance. Nothing fazes him. I only end up embarrassing myself.

I can't help but feel that it's deliberate. Surely even the laws of coincidence wouldn't condone having me put so close to him? Okay, so I'm not in the cell directly underneath him – that would have been taking things a bit too far – but we're still in viewing distance. He's only a diagonal away.

But, somehow, my life has to go on.

The doors released just as we were finishing our morning ablutions, such as they are. Time for breakfast – such as it is. In the twentieth century (once my specialist subject, fact fans), they had this idea, probably based on astronaut food, that in the future people would just eat a nutrition pill and that would be it. No chocolate, no cake, no ice cream, no pizza and chips. Boy, they expected the future to be dull. They'd have loved this place. Well, the rations aren't actually pills, they're slabs of chewy grey stuff that tastes of armpit-flavoured cardboard. Three times a day, all the protein, vitamins and minerals we need. Sometimes I even think longingly of Jason's cooking.

Claire refused to eat for the first two days. Not because the food's disgusting – although it quite obviously is – but because Pakhars are a very clean, private sort of people. I tried to rig up a tent around the facilities for her with the blanket off my bunk, but the Aseks tore it down and hit Claire for good measure. On the third day, as I was going down the corridor on my way to breakfast – having again failed to persuade Claire to join me – I heard a door slam shut. We weren't due to be shut in again until the afternoon. I ran back, and saw two Aseks holding Claire down on the floor of our cell, while a third shoved a nutrition block down her throat. She was choking on it.

I thumped on the door and screamed and yelled, but Claire couldn't hear me and after half a minute more Aseks came and dragged me to the dining room.

But during that half-minute I could see Daglan Straklant staring down through the ceiling at me, and laughing. He was still there later, when I was allowed to come back, and the cell door was unlocked again. I had to turn my face away as I hugged poor shaken Claire, because I'm not going to let him see me cry.

Claire eats now.

We queued up at the food dispenser. 'Muesli, toast and jam, black coffee, please,' I said when it was my turn. I say it every morning, with slight variations. It's not very funny, but it makes Claire smile. I think she sees it as proving I'm still me, that I'm not letting the bastards grind me down. It doesn't really prove anything of the sort, but I'd rather she didn't know that. Right at the beginning – but after the force-feeding incident – Claire tried to tell the Aseks that I needed extra rations, what with me eating for two. They ignored her. Now she always gives me half of hers, claiming she needs less as she's smaller than me. Again, I had to accept. Claire is the most utterly selfless person I know, and I couldn't hurt her by refusing. And, actually, those first few days, I had been feeling pretty weak. I think the little guy inside me has a big appetite – nothing but extreme nutritional need could make extra grey bleurgh seem like a good idea.

To my extreme irritation, the only places left this morning were on a bench with some of the cultists. Claire and I took them reluctantly, keeping our eyes only on each other or the food. Unfortunately, the cultists aren't very good at taking hints. I was next to dippy-hippy Marianne – the one who arrived the day after us and who's attached blanket-bows to her prison smock – and she immediately jumped up and curtseyed to me. 'Greetings, Great Mother,' she gushed.

I ignored her. It's the only thing to do unless you want to get into a major theological argument, which I might have been able to cope with at lunchtime, but not this early. I distracted myself by gazing underfoot to see what the inhabitants of C floor were having for breakfast today. As far as I could tell, they were having grey cardboard rations too. And I couldn't make out much of what was going on with the insect-sized folk of B floor because of the floor in between us, but I would have been prepared to bet on yummy nutrition blocks. Nice to see there's no discrimination, at least. I wondered if I should maybe wave my breakfast in the air, in case there was someone up on E floor who was also trying to make a comparative nutritional study.

Marianne didn't take the hint. 'I trust you are well, Great Mother,' she said.

'Oh yes,' I replied. 'Sometimes I almost forget I'm in prison and think I'm at a health farm.'

The cult doesn't seem to do sarcasm. She smiled. 'Then I am very pleased for you!'

Claire and I exchanged 'give me a break' looks, and we ate our cardboard as quickly as possible.

'The controls aren't responding! Damn it, what's happening?'

'Benny, these lights are flashing! What does that mean?'

'Oh goddess! We're entering military airspace! And I can't turn it round!'

'Will they shoot at us?'

'Probably. Try and get someone on the comms. Tell them we're not hostile.'

'It's not working! Benny, I'm scared!'

'Everything's gone dead! We're going down! Joseph – can you access the controls?'

'Unfortunately not, Professor Summerfield. I appear to have been locked out.'

'How is that possible?!'

'There are several ways that it could occur, including but not limited to mechanical, electronic or computer malfunction, outside interference either accidental or deliberate, the sudden development of sentience by the flight deck –'

'Goddess, do you really think that's it?'

'No.'

'Oh.'

'Taking into account the level of technology needed plus the number of confirmed incidences of spontaneous intelligence in space vehicles, I would estimate the likelihood as seventeen billion, one hundred and twenty-two million and eleven to three.'

'Well, it doesn't do to overlook a chance, however remote... Um, hello desk, you're a very nice desk, my name's Benny and this is my friend Claire, would you mind awfully taking us out of hostile airspace before we get shot?'

(Pause.)

'Nothing.'

'Benny, I still can't get a response! What do we do? What do we do?'

'Just hold on tight to something. Keep trying the comms. I'll keep trying the controls. Joseph, keep an electronic ear open for, you know, electronic stuff. If we all stay calm, everything'll be okay. We're going to be okay.'

When we got back to our cell after breakfast, there was a Grel on the other top bunk. The Grel are... an unusual race. They have faces full of quivering tentacles, and they're single minded in the search for knowledge, not tending to care what stands in their way, be it laws, people, me...

'Oh, wonderful,' I said. Those who knew me well may have been able to tell by my tone of voice that I didn't mean that literally. 'A Grel. So, are you a nice Grel or a nasty Grel? Of course, there's only about a one-in-a-thousand chance of the former, and seeing as you're in a prison...'

'Benny, we're in a prison,' Claire interrupted.

'Yes,' I explained reasonably, 'but we don't have the initial disadvantage of being Grel.'

'Aren't you being a bit... well, a bit prejudiced?' Claire said.

'The Grel have often tried to kill me!' I informed her.

'Humans have often tried to kill you,' she countered.

Sometimes, Claire is too reasonable for her own good. I hate it when she justifiably points out my character flaws. 'Besides,' she continued, 'I think she's crying...'

I looked. Claire was right. From just above me, a solitary tear dripped off a tentacle and splashed on to the smooth floor.

'I'm sorry,' I said to the Grel. Let no one say I can't be reasonable. After all I have met some reasonable Grel in my life. And they're not usually actively hostile unless they think you're withholding information from them. 'It's horrible being in here, I know. You must be new.'

The Grel sat up on the bunk. More tears dripped down. 'Bad fact: I am very miserable!' she sobbed.

'I'm Claire,' Claire told her, 'and this is Benny. What's your name?'

'I am Sophia of the Glorious Grel!'

'Hello Sophia,' I said, thinking, *Sophia*???

'Additional fact: this is my adopted name when dealing with non-Grellor races. Inferior races such as human or pakhar are not permitted the knowledge of Grellor nomenclature.' She flubbered her facial tentacles in a way I took to be analogous to a human giving themselves a pulling-yourself-together shake. 'Matter of pride: I am an expert in the etymology and usage of human names. I chose the name "Sophia" as it means "wisdom", for which I as a Grel am searching.'

'Oh,' I said, not entirely sure what to say, but glad that she'd stopped crying. I didn't take the 'inferior races' thing personally. Grel just tend to be like that. 'Well, welcome aboard, Sophia.'

At that she started howling again. 'Fact: this is a terrible place! I do not feel welcome! And they have taken my dataxe!'

Well, that was one thing to be thankful for. A dataxe was like a hideous combination of weapon and notebook: if you stuck it in someone's head it would note down all the facts from their minds for you. Unfortunately it also left a large hole in both skull and brain. A Grel doesn't go anywhere without one.

I desperately wanted to ask Sophia what she was doing in prison. Unfortunately, I had discovered there is rather a long list of unwritten rules in gaol, seemingly based on the adage 'honour among thieves'. One of these is 'thou shalt not ask what anyone's in for'. If they want to talk about it they can (some, like Gripper, being more than willing to), but you mustn't pry. A difficult stricture for a naturally curious person such as myself, and, I suspected, probably impossible for a knowledge-seeker like a Grel. Hoped I wouldn't have to be the one to explain the 'rules' to Sophia.

Claire reached up as if to pat Sophia's hand, but couldn't quite reach. She gave me a look. Reluctantly, I patted Sophia's hand in her place. 'There, there,' I said awkwardly. Sophia stopped crying again, and looked down at me.

'Query: you are engaged in the human reproductive process?' she asked.

I thought for a second. 'Yes,' I said. 'You put it so... elegantly.'

'Further query: are you therefore the carrier of the prophesied "Child of Two Mothers", known to be in this prison?' She had stopped sobbing completely now, and was looking almost eager.

I snatched my hand away and stomped over to my own bunk. 'You could have mentioned you were part of that stupid cult before I was tempted to be nice to you.'

I wasn't looking, but I heard Sophia jump off her bunk. 'Fact: you are mistaken!' she cried, coming over towards me. 'There is no empirical evidence to justify the adherence to unprovable predictions of the future. The percentage of prophesies which have been matched by some similar occurrence in the future is in fact less than that which would be expected by mere chance alone, and thus I cannot –'

'All right all right all right! I get the picture!' I said, turning to face her. 'But you obviously know all about it.'

Her tentacles wobbled in assent. 'Fact: I have heard no less than twenty-seven separate accounts of said prophecy since arriving on Deirbhile.'

Claire and I exchanged glances. 'Then for goodness' sake, would you tell us about it?' I pleaded. 'No one will tell us anything.'

Understatement (as a Grel might say): crikey.

I present the following in my own words, not Sophia's, because there's a limit to the number of colons any one person can bring herself to use. Also, I prefer not to use such phrases as 'for the glory of the Grel!', for although I acknowledge Claire's point about racial prejudice I still find myself unhappy with the whole Grel/glory thing based on various past experiences. But although these are my own words, I am attempting to tell the story factually, with no endless personal editorials. As you'll guess from the subject matter, though, it's not easy…

When I arrived at the prison, to my intense surprise it turned out that the people unofficially in charge of my bit of it were part of some cult or other. I've found out since that this cult is a big thing on Deirbhile – an important part of the resistance movement. Anyway, right from the beginning the cultists addressed me as 'Great Mother' and exempted me from all the hassley bits that go with prison life, such as kowtowing to them, paying them protection money and so on. I had assumed that they were just really fond of babies. As time went on, though, it was clear that there was a lot more too it than that. The phrase 'child of two mothers' cropped up, and there were whispers about prophecies. But the Wolf seemed annoyed enough that those bits had got out, and we weren't having much luck finding out anything more.

Maybe they were just worried I'd laugh at them if I knew the rest of it. Because, let's face it, it's pretty darn ludicrous.

Way back in the mists of time, long before the Fifth Axis was even a glint in the Imperator's eye, a woman arrived on

Deirbhile. Her name isn't recorded, she's just known as 'the Mother'. She gathered the people of Deirbhile around her, and told them that one day a terrible threat would come upon them, threatening the lives and liberty of all Deirbhilans. But a baby would be born to lead them to freedom once more, and they would know the baby in this way: it would be the child of two mothers in the year that crossed worlds. Anyway, they worked out – from a bit more info than that, but Sophia hadn't been able to track down the details – that the 'year that crossed worlds' was that grey area where the year ends in 00 (Deirbhile goes by Earth standard) and half the galaxy thinks we're at the start of a new century while the more mathematically-inclined other half insists it's the end of the old one.

A year such as 2600. Which just happens to be now.

'A child of two mothers.' That was a trickier one. There are species where reproduction includes multiple fertilisation, and there is, of course, surrogate motherhood, but the gist of the prophecy was that the 'two mothers' bit was supposed to be some incredible, unrepeatable twist of fate, not a reasonably accepted way of producing offspring.

It baffled their scholars for ages. But then some clever clogs came up with the following barmy idea: what if the mother who conceived the child was in fact *two different people*. Such as, for example, a woman who genetically became pregnant while someone else's mind was in her body. Of course, this was dismissed as unlikely. Mind-swapping was the subject of fantasies and folk tales, not reality.

Sounding familiar at all?

And I don't know who told them about me. As far as I know, only a very few people know the true circumstances behind my pregnancy. Some know about the mind-swap thing, some know about my being up the duff (after all, it's not something you can keep a secret for long), but the only people who know about both are me (obviously), Brax, Adrian, Jason, Avril (a recluse) and now Claire. Oh, and Ms

Jones and Mister Crofton. And Wolsey. And Joseph. But no one's talking about it. It's not the sort of thing you just happen to bring up in conversation.

And here's the really, really scary thing. The cult ('The Way of the Mother', way to go with a catchy title, guys), had obviously been on the alert recently, what with it being an '00' year and Deirbhile being well and truly under the yoke of oppression and desperate for a saviour, but Sophia says they didn't find out about me until recently. And that was when they *arranged for me to be brought to Deirbhile*.

I don't know how that could be. It was my decision to leave the Braxiatel Collection. The path I took was my choice. I suppose that I can see how it would have been possible to knobble my shuttle via remote control when I got near Fifth Axis airspace, and then to lead it towards Deirbhile – but the cult would need pretty high-up technology for that, which I can't see them having, and then why wasn't I shot down by the Axis on approach? Could the cult have allies in the Fifth Axis? It doesn't seem likely.

There are too many questions and nowhere near enough satisfying answers. As Sophia agrees. You can tell she's almost in physical pain not being able to get out there and research things.

The three of us discussed it all morning. I'm of the firm opinion that prophecy is bollocks, and anything that does happen to be accurate is a result of either (a) blind chance, or (b) a time-traveller having mentioned something he or she shouldn't have. And there's not as much of that stuff going on nowadays as there once was (will be? – time travel plays merry hell with your tenses). Claire is what I'd describe as a cautious sceptic. She's prepared to believe that there are 'more things in heaven and earth...' and she'll give most things a fair chance, so she won't say an outright 'no'. And apart from an enduring (and almost endearing) belief in Slawcor, the afterlife heaven where all facts are known, Sophia will believe only those things which are incontrovertibly proved to her. So between us the general opinion was that I was *not* the Great Mother, bearer of this prophesied child. But consensus also was that as the cult obviously believed I was, it was still something that had to be dealt with.

It was the 'being brought to Deirbhile' bit that was still sticking with me. Sophia was adamant that this was what she had heard, and from a number of separate sources. And while I acknowledged that perhaps it was all a bit much to be a coincidence, I still couldn't see how it was done.

DAY −7, AFTERNOON

I made an even greater attempt than usual to keep out of the way of the cult at lunchtime. Oh, I definitely wanted to talk to them at some point. But I wanted to have all my questions ready first.

We were locked in as usual through the afternoon, and the three of us avoided talking about you-know-what because of Gripper. Claire insisted I had an after-lunch nap. I didn't feel up to arguing with her, but my mind was buzzing too much to sleep. I lay there with my eyes shut, thinking.

DAY −7, EVENING

By the end of the afternoon I knew I was going to have to talk to the Wolf and her chums, whether I knew the right questions to ask or not. But when we got to the dining hall in the evening, I couldn't get anywhere near her. The room was overflowing with new people, and they were all swarming around the Wolf.

'There's never been this big an intake all at once,' Deedee from next door whispered to me, as we hovered near the doorway, waiting for a path to clear to the food dispenser.

'Fact: they were in the holding cells when I arrived this morning,' Sophia just happened to mention.

'What?' I said. 'All of them?'

'Confirmation: that is so. Additional information: they were subject to…' her voice broke slightly, '…much interrogation, some of which I was forced to witness.'

'If they've been kept down there all day…' I looked again. A few of the women weren't joining in the general crowding-round, they were sitting down and staring at nothing. If they had been being interrogated all day… well, it wasn't something I cared to imagine.

You have to understand that this is horrendously difficult for me. I fight for things. I fight for people's rights; for justice; for freedom. I get oppressed masses to rally round me. I expose scandals for all the world to see.

But I can't do that here.

I know that there's injustice here. There are the interrogations. The lack of privacy. The rations that, okay, ensure we don't die from malnutrition, but which mean we have a constant, nagging hunger. And the force-feeding. Sounds ridiculous, doesn't it? We suffer from hunger and force-feeding. Yeah, what a joke. Food is a powerful weapon. The person who controls it controls everyone – you're not allowed to choose your own destiny. Stop eating, they force it down your throat. And of course if you play up the Aseks in any way, you suddenly find that your cell door remains closed the next morning while everyone else's automatically opens. And then you'll have to spend the next twenty-four hours with three starving cell mates who don't see why they should pay the price for your behaviour. A sort of self-regulation. Very clever on behalf of the authorities. Gits that they are.

It all seems a bit contradictory, but what it boils down to is that they're asserting their control over us.

I'm wandering from my point. The point is: I can't do anything about this. Yes, there's injustice. What does one normally do in this sort of situation? I'll tell you. Fight it. Tell the authorities. Tell the public. Create outrage, force a change. But how can I fight? And who am I going to expose this to? Everyone knows! There's no Fifth Axis propaganda machine telling the Deirbhilans they're just borrowing their planet for a little while. There's no belief outside the Assimilated Territories that the Axis are being nice to all the people they conquer. I know as well as anyone about the massacres, the concentration camps, the alien-cleansing policies. And what did I do about it? I sat on my comfy little planetoid eating chocolate-chip ice cream and enjoying the view.

Could I organise an uprising? Prisoners against the imprisoners! Well, I probably could. And then...?

You can't get out of the Glass Prison. And even if you did, you'd be shot on sight. And even if you weren't, you can't get off the planet. And even if you did, they'd shoot you down. And even if they didn't... The Fifth Axis wasn't going to go away.

And I have to think of my baby.

Normally, I'll take risks with things. Not worry. Everything will turn out all right in the end, that sort of thing. But now... I have complete and utter responsibility for someone else's life. And someone who – totally illogically as I've never met them, and they're hardly in much of a position to have impressed me with their personality – I love more than life itself. Weird, huh?

Even if I still don't know if it's mine.

There was a sudden shout from the head of the food-machine queue. 'It's all gone!'

What? They never ran out of food! And did I mention how hungry you got in here?

There were a few annoyed grumbles, getting louder and louder as people worked out what was going on. Soon there were shouts. *Bastards! Feed us! Give us food! We need food!*

'There are too many people!' Claire whispered. 'They've not increased the number of rations!'

I saw a small plump woman punching her fist in the air – the Wolf. If she was happy to stir up the problem rather than calm it down, we were in trouble. There were a lot of tensions that needed relieving.

Tables and benches were attached to the floor, but there were still things to throw – plastic beakers, jugs, plates. Some of the women were even throwing shoes at each other. Rather them than me – they'd probably never get them back, and shoes were one of our few personal possessions.

There were the usual few Aseks standing round the walls. Aseks don't carry weapons – nothing that could be taken by a prisoner and used against them, you see – but they're strong, and there's no rule that says they can't use violence. A slab of foodstuff hit one of them on its ghostly white cheek and it didn't blink an eyelid; didn't bother to wipe it off. (Now that's typically illogical behaviour on behalf of the prisoners – riot about not having enough food and waste the stuff that you do have.) The Asek stalked forward, gunk dripping from its chin, and grabbed the thrower by her arm. It was Deedee, the girl from the cell next door. She was screaming, trying to prise up the Asek's strong fingers, and as I started towards her the creature threw her to the floor. She was going to get trampled.

This all happened in seconds. I'd only got a step forward when I felt Claire's hand on my arm. 'Benny, you have to get out of here,' she squeaked above the shouts and screams of the other prisoners.

And here's another instance of that thing I keep on about (sorry to repeat myself so often). I wouldn't normally have listened to her; I'd have waded in there to help out. But I had to think about my baby. I stopped, and turned my back on Deedee.

'All right,' I said. A shoe came our way and caught Claire on the arm, hard enough to make her give a little gasp of breath. I took her hand and began to pull her towards the door...

...and the world rushed over my head. I was falling... I was hurting...

'Benny! Hold on – I'll get help!' Claire was squeaking, alarmed, but the room was spinning and she seemed to be

30

fading away – and then there were feet, noisy feet, stamping feet… I could hear cries and shouts – Aseks and prisoners. There seemed to be a lot of fighting going on, far away. A faint cry above it all: 'The mother! The mother!' Suddenly arms were grabbing me from all sides and I was being dragged to my feet – and then my legs were lifted too, and I was being taken away. And all I could think was, my baby! Have they hurt my baby!

I was lying flat out on my bunk, and I had an audience. If I'd been charging admission, I'd have made enough to buy a whole box of combs and had enough left over for a toothbrush. I realised that the people who'd been carrying me were Sophia, Jevina from next door, Marianne and, surprisingly, Gripper. She hadn't really struck me as the caring sort up till then, you know, what with being an assassin and all. There were a lot of new faces in the cell too, some of them kneeling. Can a face kneel? Oh, you know what I mean. There were looks of reverence all around.

'Are you all right, Great Mother?' Marianne breathed.

I didn't want to answer that just yet. I wasn't completely sure. 'What happened?' I asked.

Sophia answered. 'Alarming fact: there was insufficient food! The guards attempted to quell the protests, and knocked you to the floor!'

I suddenly realised there was a face missing. 'Claire!' I cried, trying to get up.

Marianne pushed at my shoulder. 'Do not disturb yourself, Great Mother. You must rest!'

'Bollocks to that!' I shouted, slapping her hand away. 'What's happened to Claire?' I tried to jump off the bunk, but couldn't quite manage it. I hung like a giant wobbling jelly in the air for a moment, and then plummeted back to bed. I hit out in frustration; Marianne ducked back to avoid my flailing arms. 'I don't want to be an elephant!' I yelled. 'I have to get to Claire. I *have* to get to *Claire*!'

There seemed to be hands coming from everywhere trying

to stroke me; voices softly telling me to calm down, they'd find Claire for me. I was almost weeping – bloody hormones. I didn't want to be comforted. I didn't want people to sort things out for me. I wanted to be able to do it myself!

It was several painful minutes before one of the cultists returned. 'It's all over,' she said. 'No one left.'

'Claire?' I asked.

'No one left,' she said. 'Everyone's back in their cells. The rest have been taken to A floor.'

I struggled into a sitting position. 'But have they taken Claire?'

'The important thing is that you and our child are all right, Great Mo–' the woman began.

I was sick of this. 'No, that is *not* the most important thing. The most important thing is that my friend has been dragged off somewhere! And this –' I patted my belly, 'is bloody well *my* child and no one else's. How *dare* you stand there and claim my child is your property! I am *not* your "Great Mother", your prophecy is a load of balls and THIS IS MY BABY! Now, GET OUT!'

The women looked a bit shocked. They're probably not used to prophecies answering them back. Marianne began to bustle them out of the cell – but I saw her expression. It was a 'humour her' look.

'I am not joking,' I told her. 'I don't know what rubbish you believe, I don't know whether you really did drag me to your goddess-forsaken planet somehow, but you are never, *never* going to have anything to do with my child.'

She beamed at me. 'You cannot escape destiny, Great Mother.' Lucky for her I had all the agility of a blancmange, or I'd have plastered her saintly smile all over her smug chops.

I managed to get to my feet, with Sophia's help. I think she'd have rather I stayed on the bunk, but was a bit scared of me at the moment. There was an Asek in the corridor outside. 'Back!' it barked at us.

'I just want to find out about my friend…'

'Back!' It came at us, expressionless.

I stood firm.

'Get in your cell.'

'Could you just tell me about –'

It raised its arm. I snapped. I pushed it out of the way, and ran down the corridor.

Ran *very slowly* down the corridor.

By the time I reached the shut-off elevator that led to the lower floors, a whole bunch of Aseks had caught up with me. I think it was only the baby that let me off without a beating. They just dragged me back to my cell, heels grazing the floor, threw me in and watched the cell door clang shut. Early lock-in.

Again, the baby saves me. Of course, if it wasn't for the baby, I wouldn't be in this mess.

I've never felt so bloody helpless. And then I looked up, and saw that Daglan Straklant had been watching it all.

Flat on my bunk, it all drained away. I was helpless. I was vulnerable. I was alone. Despite my ireful protestations to the cultists, I was suddenly hit with the worst lot of doubts yet. This wasn't my baby. This was the baby of Avril Fenman, witch. I was being put through all this for some evil spawn thing. Growing inside my body was an alien thing, sucking my life force, leeching my energy. I *hated* it. Hated it so much I had to force myself to keep utterly still, because I knew that if I moved I would freak and try to rip it out of me somehow. If I had a blade I could slice open my stomach and then I could squeeze the thing out and turn over and curl up in a corner and forget all about it for ever. I was holding my breath and didn't dare let it out.

It was over an hour before anyone in our cell spoke. I'd been lying on my bunk, eyes wide open, unmoving, staring at the underside of Claire's bed for sixty whole minutes. It wasn't fair that they'd taken her. None of this was fair at all.

I accepted this baby. I had to. If I didn't…

Sophia broke the silence. 'Query...?' she said nervously.

'Mm?' I replied.

'Um... query with intention of distraction: are you informed as to the chromosomal idiosyncrasy of your foetus?'

I thought for a few moments. 'Do you mean, do I know if it's a boy or a girl?'

'Confirmation of query: yes.'

I took a deep breath. Back to normality. This was my baby, and I would act accordingly.

'I don't know, actually,' I said. 'I mean, I suppose I could have found out had I wanted to, but it didn't cross my mind. Of course, I want to know – but all in good time. It's like how you shake the presents under the Christmas tree – you like the thrill of guessing, but it ruins everything if you actually work it out. Or like reading the end of a whodunit first. I suppose I just like to get the full experience every time.' I thought again. 'Actually, I'm not sure if that makes sense, even to me. Maybe it's part of my... denial thing. I've just been thinking of it – as "it".'

'Fact: in many tribes of Africa on Earth, a baby was referred to only as "it", or perhaps "thing" until it had been formally named.'

I was surprised. 'You really do know about human names, then?'

'Good fact,' she confirmed. 'Query relating to specialisation: have you decided upon a nomenclature for your child?'

'Have I thought of a name? No. No, I haven't. I suppose I'll just see what it looks like, and decide then.'

Sophia mouth-tentacles began to quiver. 'The naming is most important! A name must fit its bearer! It must be considered at great length!'

'Well, I suppose I agree,' I told her, thinking again of my friend Chlamydia and her blighted life. 'Go on, then, dazzle me with appropriate names.'

(I decided not to mention the Killoran tradition of

34

adopting human names with a military connection. My baby was not growing up with a warrior complex. It had been bad enough when Adrian kept coming round to read Killoran battle poetry to my womb – especially as that was complicated by the fact that he wasn't actually speaking to *me* at the time. Being quite pro the rights of the father I didn't feel I could stop him, but, not being entirely comfortable with my baby absorbing war-loving propaganda, after each of his sessions I started declaiming Wilfred Owen and Siegfried Sassoon. I'm slightly worried that I may have a confused child.)

So I lay there and listened to a high-pitched Grel voice telling me of Roberts and Coinneachs and Myffanwys. Names of valour, or godliness, or just happening to look a bit like something else.

All in all, it had been an odd day.

3
The Name Game

Names. They have an incredible significance. It's not for nothing that many magical traditions consider knowing a person's name to be akin to having power over them. Just look at Rumpelstiltskin. Once someone knows your name, you can never hide from them, not completely. From the vidphone sales-person who greets you 'Hello Benny', when they've never met you, to the policeman who says 'Bernice Surprise Summerfield, I am arresting you for...', they own a part of you.

Look at the people in my cell. How many of their true names do I know?

Sophia. It was one of the first things she told us; that non-Grel couldn't know Grel names. I have no idea what she's really called.

Gripper. Her real name might be Agrippina. (Sophia tried to explain to me exactly how Roman names worked, but it all got a bit confusing, what with praenomen, nomen, cognomen and goddess knows how many other bits, some of which a female was allowed and some of which she wasn't, and how all the children in a Roman family would have the same name or something.) But let's assume that Gripper's real name is something else, because I'm pretty sure of it. This means that she chose to take a name other than her own, and what's more one famously born by a woman who allegedly poisoned her husband (that's the emperor Claudius, fact fans – or, to illustrate my point further, Tiberius Claudius Drusus Nero Germanicus to be exact). So she's telling us she's notorious and she's probably a killer.

But then she takes it even further. From her elegant but deadly alias, she goes on to adopt a nickname. One that sounds more like something you'd give to a scary tattooed man or a rotweiller. So she's now telling us she's tough and mean and not to be messed with.

We get told all that – but we still don't know her real name. We can't touch her.

Claire. The best example I could give of the power of names. See elsewhere for its effect on me. Would I have still hired Claire even if she hadn't been wonderful? Well no, probably not. But there's no denying that name gave her an advantage on some level. And of course it isn't her real name either, just the humanised version of it. She's really Clair'atil.

So out of the four people in D21, the only one who uses her proper name is me!

Or do I? I'm Bernice Surprise Summerfield. But I think of myself as Benny. And I'm commonly known as Professor Summerfield. My name wasn't enough, so I adopted a title. (Before I was academically entitled to, I admit, but now it's perfectly legitimate.) I was hiding my true nature, pretending to be something I wasn't. And I did it through my name. And then, of course, there was the brief period where I became Professor Bernice Surprise Summerfield-Kane. What's that telling people? 'I am important. I am an individual. I have a connection to another person, but won't let it eclipse my identity.' There's no clearer way of severing your connection with a person than dropping their name...

When Claire and Isaac sat down with a stack of 'Name Your Baby' books, did they have the slightest idea what I'd end up being called? I could have become a 'Bernie'. Or a 'B.S'. *'Hey, B.S.!' 'How ya doin', Bernie?'* Ugh, sounds so wrong, doesn't it? But just a few different turns along the way, and that could have been me.

Incidentally, I am known to my cat as 'servant woman'. Cats obviously know well the art of naming a person for what they are.

Let's look at some other people. The Wolf, for example. Did she adopt the name or was it thrust upon her? Doesn't matter. Still don't know her real name. She's telling us how she wants to be seen. An animal. A ruthless predator.

The Aseks. We don't know their names. We don't even know if they have names. We can barely tell them apart through appearance and definitely not through personality or mannerisms, and we have no official labels to give them. So we have no power over them. We can't tell if the one we spoke to at lunchtime is the same one who pushed past us in the corridor just before lock-up.

I have friends who've never revealed their names to a single soul, and others who've been known by nicknames their whole lives. I knew people who abandoned parts of their names for ideological reasons, and others who insist on mispronouncing their names, which both avoids and creates confusion. But I also know several people whose names are barely pronounceable, and completely impossible to spell. Tell me, do you think '!' is an acceptable letter of the alphabet?

Irving Braxiatel may really be called Irving Braxiatel – though I admit to not knowing that for a fact – but you can tell the degree of familiarity between us because I call him Brax and he calls me Benny. And the less said about Adrian Wall, or his friends Alexander Thegrate and Nelson Scolumn, the better.

My friend Keri (also a Pakhar) is really Ker'a'nol.

Jason almost gets away unscathed, but there was the abortive 'Kane-Summerfield' incident.

Mister Crofton – well, no one knows his first name.

Ms Jones – I once heard that her given name was Cleopatra, but I think that may have been a joke of some sort. Call her 'Miss' or 'Mrs' Jones, however, and face her wrath. She will give you no clues. You get to find out no intimate details about her life.

Even Daglan Straklant is defined for me by his title – his rank, Kolonel – even though he no longer bears it.

I'm trying to think of a single person I know who is known by one true name alone. For a moment I thought of Wolsey. And then realised that he was once known as 'Power Puss', has been 'Puss in Boots', and although he never mentioned

39

it, the other cats probably call him 'Fearsome Catcher of Mice and Drinker of Cream' or something.

You know, that's a pretty good system that I'm fictionally attributing to cats, there. It's rather like the tradition of certain tribes of the Native Americans on Earth. You are not defined by your name, your name is defined by you. A Native American could have numerous names throughout his life, and be known by all of them at the same time, to different people. Goodness knows what I'd have been called over the years if I were a Native American. 'Wears Big Earrings.' 'Fell-off-a-cliff.' 'Traveller in Mysterious Box.' 'Throws Plates at Husband.' 'Drinks Students Under Table.' 'Not as Young as She Was.' 'Younger Than She Was.' 'Locked in Prison on Alien World While Pregnant and Hopeless.' Just trips off the tongue.

But the whole system of names is almost unbelievable. Look at that list up there: Bernice; Jason; Irving; Claire; Adrian. It's almost the twenty-seventh century, we're light years from Earth, and over fifty per cent of us are known by names derived from ancient Earth Hebrew or Indo-European roots. (This was a 'fact!' from Sophia.) How many people over the last thousand years or so have thought about what a name is symbolising, rather than just what it sounds like? I've known a Melanie ('black') with porcelain skin and abundant red locks, a completely celibate Annie ('blessed with child') and an atheist Christopher.

In earlier years, children were named for physical attributes, or moral or intellectual qualities that they either possessed, or, more commonly, that their elders hoped they would grow to possess. The name had a mystic significance – if you labelled your child as brave or clever or close to God, then the universe would know that that was what they should be and arrange it accordingly. I am not superstitious, but I do believe there is something in this. One of my pretty shrewd judgements of human psychology, that would be – a name can shape a child. 'Sticks and stones will break my bones, but words will never hurt me', said Ugly Dung-for-

Brains Cowardly Greasy Zitface. But he was misinformed.

4
Something Wicked This Way Comes

DAY –6, MORNING

I jumped out of bed as soon as I woke up the next morning – all right, eased myself slowly up if you want to be pedantic – splashed cold water over my face, and then paced the floor until they released the doors. To my utter relief, Claire was waiting for me inside the dining room.

She ran over as soon as she saw me, and hugged my thighs (that's not really relevant or indicative of anything but our relative heights. She's not a thigh-fetishist or anything). She was smiling, but I got the feeling that it was a brave smile for my benefit. 'What did they do to you?' I asked her softly, stroking her fur.

The smile wobbled a bit. 'Please, Benny, I don't want to talk about it. I'm all right now. That's all that matters.'

'I tried to come after you…'

'I knew you would. But they took everyone down to A floor. There were about ten of us.' She shivered. 'I really don't want to talk about it. Not yet.'

So I didn't ask her any more. She didn't let go of my hand until we'd got our rations and sat down, though.

There were enough rations for everyone this morning. I did wonder what had brought about the sudden massive intake yesterday that had taken the normally super-efficient administration so by surprise.

After breakfast, as we were getting up from our table, Marianne came over to us. 'Greetings, Great Mother,' she said, curtseying. That's the great thing about cultists. You can be rude to them one day, and the next day they just come back for more.

43

I folded my arms. 'Good morning, Marianne. Are you bending in that funny way to really rub in how unsupple I am at the moment? I must say, that's not very kind of you. Some might even call it insensitive.'

Her smile didn't waver. 'The Wolf would like to see you now, Great Mother.'

'Oh really? Well, I have plans. Tell her to make an appointment.'

Still no sign of the smile slipping. 'In her cell in five minutes, please. And she would like you to bring the Grel with you.'

'She has a name you know,' I told her. 'And she might have plans too.'

Marianne walked off, still smiling. There wasn't any point arguing anyway. After all, now I knew what this prophecy thing was all about, I wanted to see the Wolf probably more than she wanted to see me.

I must now explain a bit about internal prison politics. On each floor, there's a woman who's risen to the top – as per cream or scum, depending on your point of view. That woman says what goes. The rights of the individual mean little to her, unless she happens to be the individual in question. According to her lackeys, she's looking after all our interests. Yeah right, and I'm Pope Bernice the Third.

The trouble is, I personally don't have anything to complain about. Of course there are lots of general things, like not thinking she (and I'm talking about our particular floor-leader, here, obviously) should be bossing people about. I'm a big democracy person. Only trouble is, she was voted in. So that means... I'm in favour of democracy, but only when I approve of the result. A tricky one, that. I'm reasonably sure she would have intimidated people into it, though, so it wouldn't have been a fair contest. Phew – Bernice's personal ethical policy saved by a technicality.

The reason that things aren't too bad for me is that our floor-leader, known as 'The Wolf' for reasons I shall come to in a moment, is Big Chief Lady of the cult. So I am, to her, a big important prophesy figure. She isn't actually *nice* to me – not in the way that, say, Marianne always treats me with a bit of reverence – now that I know what their prophecy is saying, I'm guessing the Wolf regards me as merely a vessel in which their saviour is being temporarily carried, but of course one still has to take care of the vessel if one wants the contents to remain undamaged.

One of the Wolf's little hobbies – oh, hang on a minute, I promised to explain her name, so quick digression: looks harmless, fools others into thinking she's nice, actually pretty damn tough and ruthless inside. Wolf in sheep's clothing. Stories say the name was flung at her as an insult and she liked it so much she adopted it. Me, I think she made it up herself. Her sort do that stuff. Anyway, one of her little hobbies is a floor-wide protection racket. Cultists don't have to pay. Neither do I.

There isn't much currency around. Most prisons I've seen/been in have a fair amount of smuggling and black market stuff going on; not this one. Oh, there's been the occasional slip up, but the searches and the torture and the total lack of visitors or bribeable warders have managed to keep the place more or less clean.

So, instead, there's an internal system of credits. You gain credits by doing jobs for other prisoners (who have credits they can pass on); selling services or possessions. Claire and I didn't have anything when we were brought in, but a few of the local girls were actually allowed to keep the odd non-threatening item, like a toothbrush or comb. When a prisoner leaves – I won't say 'is released', because that's probably not what's happened – her things are claimed by the cult. If you really need something, you can probably find it at the Wolf's shop, if you have the credits to pay. The richest women on the floor (aside from the Wolf herself) are the two giant Terpsechians who exude a mild euphoria agent from – well, I'm not entirely sure from where, I'll just say 'from their bodies'.

45

Mind you, Terpsechians are so big – we're talking walrus-sized here – that this pair could probably have got a lot of people to hand over cash anyway. Not that they seem to be fierce, but some people do judge by size. As I often used to have to remind my ex-husband.

I am not in the money. I don't have anything anyone wants. I tried offering a customised haiku writing service, but had no buyers. Likewise, lectures on the history of twentieth-century Earth seem not to be a saleable commodity. Even were I willing to slave for a fellow prisoner, the cult won't let me. There is a Benny embargo – as (alleged) Great Mother I cannot stoop so low.

You might think it weird that the so-called peace-loving Way of the Mother is running the joint with threats and nastiness, while ex-members of the powerful and power-hungry Fifth Axis (such as Gripper) just sit back and watch and pay up. But I think the reason's right there. Outside, the cultists and the ordinary folk of Deirbhile had no chance, not against the Axis forces. They planned and plotted in secret, but didn't have the resources or experience to make a dent in the military.

Here, there's much more of a level playing field, and the non-Axis people have a hell of a lot to prove and a hell of a lot of scores to settle. They really have the motivation. The ex-Axis people, on the other hand, are either lone operators like Gripper, who don't seem to have any interest in seizing power and seem to find the whole thing terribly amusing, or women who are so used to their place in the scheme of things – giving or taking orders – that they can't cope now everything's been taken away from them. I dare say if just one Axis woman had decided to take charge then all the others would have rallied round and she could have put up a fairly stonking leadership challenge, but that hasn't happened. And no one else is going to rock the boat.

But, you know, that's all just guesswork. Guesswork by someone with a pretty shrewd judgement of human psychology, if I do flatter myself, but guesswork nonetheless.

Shame no one's paying for some pretty shrewd judgements of human psychology this week, though.

But although I'm exempt, Claire has to pay protection to the Wolf, and now Sophia will too. It really winds me up. Normally, you see, I'd be right out there challenging it, telling them not to pay. But I can't. For a start, I'd be asking them to risk something that I can't risk myself – I can't refuse to pay because I don't have to anyway. And I can't defend them. Oh, of course, if anything happened, I would defend them to the hilt, but as it is – well, our motto has to be 'anything for a quiet life'. I know I keep on about that. About how I should be an action person but I'm not doing anything; I seem to spend half my time justifying my behaviour to myself. If you get bored with my constant self-flagellation, please feel free to skip those bits.

Thankfully, Claire hasn't had too hard a job making the payments so far. With her medical training, she's been holding little mini-surgeries where she dispenses advice. Luckily most of the prisoners are of races whose biology she understands, although there was an incident that almost turned nasty once involving a remedy for piles – but I won't say any more because Claire would prefer it never to be mentioned or even thought of ever again.

Sophia, with her encyclopaedic memory and recent capture was able to earn a little yesterday selling information on the status of loved ones, homes and so on outside on Deirbhile. She didn't want to ask for money for doing that, but I'm afraid it was I who came up with the idea and persuaded her. 'Strike while the iron's hot,' I told her. 'It's a dog eat dog world.' And then I had to spend the rest of the afternoon sating her desire for further knowledge of the wonderful world of human aphorisms. Still, at least it took her mind off being in this stinking place for a little while.

Wish somebody'd take my mind off it.

Sophia and I presented ourselves in the Wolf's cell, Sophia nervously, me with bad grace. The Wolf's cell is almost

47

exactly like ours, two double bunks, a washstand and a loo (NB the plumbing in this place is not, thankfully, see-through. Just so you know), but there are subtle differences – the almost twee plastic beaker on the washstand containing four toothbrushes, the two blankets on the bed. She shares a cell with Marianne and two other cultists, but at the moment there were just the three of us.

Actually, the main difference between our cell and the Wolf's is the smell, or rather the lack of it. It appears to be a cell of infinite soap, a thing that only money can buy. Thank goodness I'm used to (a) sweaty archaelogical digs and (b) students, because I think someone of a more delicate temperament just wouldn't survive. Mind you, I must admit to being the main culprit in our cell – Pakhars are able to wash themselves with their tongues (although Claire, for one, would infinitely prefer a bubble bath), and Grels have that rubbery skin that doesn't seem to sweat. No, it's Ms Human Glands here who is really in need of a bar of carbolic and a scrubbing brush. This only lends credence, I believe, to my theory that the noseless Aseks were genetically-engineered especially for this job. I had previously discussed this theory with Claire and Sophia. 'My dog's got no nose,' I added.

'How does it smell?' Claire had chimed in.

'Theory: perhaps it is able to smell with its tongue in the manner of snakes and certain other reptiles?' offered Sophia before I could get in there with the punchline. 'Also, you have never previously mentioned this dog, Benny. I was aware only of the existence of your feline companion, Wolsey. I must store knowledge of this dog and its unusual nasal impairment as a new fact!'

I've really grown to love Sophia.

Here in the Wolf's cell, I resisted the urge to give my armpits a quick sniff to check how much whiff I was adding to the place. If she didn't want me stinking up her home, she could jolly well let me have some soap. You'd think the cult would want their Great Mother to be fragrant, wouldn't you? But obviously not.

The Wolf is five foot two or so and a bit chubby, looks about forty-five, and has tight curls in a mauvey shade. It's either natural for Deirbhilans or the latest fashion, because a lot of the girls have hair that colour. She wears matching lipstick: another status symbol.

I didn't say anything, waiting for her to make the first move. But I realised after a few seconds that although she was looking in my direction she wasn't actually looking at me – she was looking at my belly. I crossed my arms across it protectively, and bent my knees until I met her eyeline. I probably wouldn't be able to get up again without help, but it was worth it to see the brief flicker of annoyance that darted across her face.

'Hello,' I said. 'I don't think we've been formally introduced. I'm Professor Bernice Summerfield. And you are…?'

Her eyes narrowed. 'You may call me Wolf.'

'Fair enough,' I said. 'You may call me Professor Summerfield. And this is my friend, Sophia.'

I began to wobble on my heels, and threw myself into a sort of backwards fall into a sitting position on the bunk opposite her. I think it looked as though I'd done it deliberately. I patted the mattress beside me, indicating that Sophia should sit too. After a brief nervous look at the Wolf, she did so.

Having watched all this, the Wolf began speaking. 'I am told that thanks to this Grel –'

'– Sophia,' I filled in, in case she'd missed it.

'– you now are fully aware of your destiny.'

I creased up my forehead. 'You know, I can't say I am. Between you and me, I think I've been through my fair share of destinies already. I was quite looking forward to just staying at home, taking up beekeeping, growing vegetable marrows, something like that. Until you brought me here, that is…?' I made it a question.

…which she didn't answer. 'You had to come here. It is

49

your destiny.'

'Oh no it isn't!' I told her.

'Oh yes it... It most certainly is,' she said. 'Your child will lead us from these dark times.'

'No he won't!' I said, with rather more force than I was intending. 'Or she. Whichever. Because I am going to get out of here somehow, and my baby and I are going to keep those bees or grow those marrows together. I am sorry that your planet's been taken over, and, believe it or not, if there was anything I could do to help I would. But my baby is not being caught up in any war.'

She had a faint smile on her face. 'But you have no choice. It has been foretold.'

'Then it wasn't told very well. I'm sorry to have to tell you this, but just because something's been written in a book for a few hundred years, it doesn't mean it's true. Now I believe in a lot of things, but prophecy is not one of them. This –' I patted my tummy '– is just a baby. An ordinary baby, and up until a few months ago no one even had a clue it was going to be born. Certainly no one knows how it's going to turn out. It's special to me because it's part of me, but it's not some supernatural force. A baby can't win a war.'

'I agree with you,' she said.

That surprised me. 'You do?'

'Oh yes. We are resigned that it may be many years before we throw off our oppressors. But we have learned patience, over the years.'

Oh bollocks. 'Hang on a minute – there is no way we're hanging around for years!'

She shook her head. 'What happens to you after this child is born is irrelevant – Professor Summerfield.'

I hunched forward involuntarily, shielding my bump again.

She continued. 'This child is our greatest hope. We have seen our planet overrun by vicious criminals, the whole galaxy is about to fall to them, and –'

'What?!' I cried. 'You're exaggerating, surely.'

She smiled again, but ruefully this time. 'I'm afraid I'm not.

But I admit to not knowing all the details. I was hoping your – friend – could help me out.' She looked at Sophia. Sophia looked puzzled.

'Query?'

The Wolf crossed her legs. For a moment I thought she was going to offer us a cup of tea and a slice of cake, she looked so benevolent.

'Yesterday the Axis rounded up everyone they suspected of being a follower of the Way of the Mother. I am pleased to say that a number of our brothers and sisters are still at liberty, but also feel heartened that the enemy considers us enough of a threat to act towards us in this way.'

'Yeah, great,' I muttered. 'Really heartening, having most of your mates in prison with you. At least you won't get lonely.'

She ignored me. Probably just as well. 'The sisters who joined us yesterday report that there are rumours of a massive campaign about to begin. Many ships have been arriving over the last few days. High-ranking members of the Axis have been spotted. It's rumoured that the Imperator himself is or will be on Deirbhile.'

'Oh goddess!' I said. The Imperator. The top man. The one in charge. The one responsible for thousands upon thousands of deaths. Makes you feel a bit weird, thinking you could be within walking distance of such evil. What's even weirder is that he probably doesn't think of himself as evil at all. They never do.

The Wolf flicked a hand towards Sophia. 'I understand that you were asking a lot of questions of both followers and Axis soldiers. I want to know if you discovered anything that might have a bearing on this.'

Sophia twitched. 'Fact: nine spaceships of the Alpha class arrived on Deirbhile in the thirty-seven hours prior to my unjustified incarceration.'

'Nine *Alphas*? Are you absolutely sure?'

'It is a good fact.'

'Sounds like your information could be right,' I said to the

Wolf, trying to hide just how uncomfortable this potential news made me. 'Why didn't you mention this before?' I asked Sophia.

'Fact: no one enquired,' she said. Well, I suppose that's true. Very factual race, the Grel. Not ones for idle gossip.

So, bearing that in mind, I found myself temporarily allied with the Wolf in enquiring about as many facts as possible from Sophia. And the information we extracted did not indicate good news.

DAY –6, AFTERNOON

'It sounds like everyone who is anyone is here. They're definitely planning a major offensive. If they succeed – well, it'll change the course of everything.' I shook my head despondently.

'But there'll be resistance, surely?' Claire asked. She didn't seem to understand the import of what we were telling her.

'Claire! It's not that simple. You know what it's like out there, out there in the worlds beyond the assimilated territories. Half of them don't even know there's a war on. Those who do know about it – it's somebody else's problem. After the Kasagrad setback everyone's assumed the Axis were in retreat. They won't be expecting this at all.'

And that's not the worst of it, I thought. Planets that don't have much technology will be overrun. Planets that do have a reasonable military presence will try and fight – but they'll be unprepared and the Axis will wipe the floor with them. And all the ones in between… Take the Braxiatel Collection, for instance. It's not as though it's even a planet, but I'm betting they'll still target it for the wealth it contains. All Brax's security measures – passes, clearance levels, restricted transport – it'll all count for naught. It's all very well having a security disk encoded to individual bio-emissions, but if you've got a big enough gun you can just blow the door away. So you've got a fleet of military warships heading towards you, and all you've got on your side is Mister

Crofton with a shovel and Adrian Wall with a pickaxe. Oh, and Ms Jones with a sharpened tongue, which is probably the only weapon that might give them pause for thought.

I'm going to be in prison for the rest of my life, they're going to take my baby away, and all my friends are soon going to be killed. It's enough to make anyone slightly miffed. I blinked back a few hormonal tears.

'We have to get a message out,' I said. 'Somehow, we have to alert people. If we can't stop it going ahead – and to be perfectly honest I don't see how we possibly can – then at least we can do our very best to stop it being such a complete walkover.'

'Query: how?' Sophia asked. Of course, that was the six million credit question.

I thought about it for a few minutes. If only I could get hold of Joseph, my handy porter and communications device – but they'd taken him away from me within seconds of our crash landing. 'There must be some sort of comms on A floor,' I said. 'We just have to get to it, somehow.'

'Unfortunate fact: not so,' said Sophia. 'The Glass Prison is set within a communications exclusion zone for additional security. All Asek orders are given in person.'

'Bugger,' I said. 'Bugger, bugger, bugger. That knocks that one on the head, then. We're hardly going to be able to persuade an Asek to smuggle out a message to an opposing power.'

'Fact: we must think of something!' said Sophia. And of course, I agreed with her. But like so many things, it was easier said than done...

5
Hanging With
the Enemy

DAY –6, EVENING

In some ways it almost made things better. Having some big, galaxy-threatening thing to worry about, I mean. You see, I can do that. I've been there before. When it's something that big – well, you just know it'll all turn out all right in the end. It always does; it has to. Universal laws, or something. But when it's something small – your baby, your liberty, even your life – things don't seem quite so certain. The laws don't have to be on your side.

Ridiculous, isn't it? I was lying in bed trying to use thoughts of a galactic war and the assimilation of numerous worlds to distract me from the night-time terrors of my own situation. The thought of being in here for ever. Of them taking away my baby. Of Straklant. Of what Straklant might do to me if he got the chance. Of what Straklant might do to my baby.

I could hear little snuffly snores coming from Claire, and, if I listened carefully, two sets of heavy breathing from the other bunk. I was the only one awake.

Well, the only one in here.

Only the barest hint of moonlight filtered through the seven ceilings between me and the night sky, but I could still make out movements in the gloom. One of the women in the far side cell got up for a drink of water. Deedee, separated from me only by a transparent wall, was tossing and turning in her sleep. I think she had nightmares most nights.

I almost reached out to her, to comfort her, thinking the gesture might mean something despite the barriers. But

I realised – strangely, to my surprise – that I was frozen. I didn't dare move. I was convinced that Straklant would be sitting up there, watching out for me. I knew, abstractly, that I was giving him a position of power over me by allowing even the thought of him to dictate my actions (I mean, he was probably tucked under his blankets fast asleep!), but now it was there I just couldn't get it out of my head… It was like watching a horror vid. Even if you were half-expecting the dead villain to suddenly reappear, it still gave you a shock when he did. If I looked up and Straklant *was* staring into our cell, I would scream the place down like a baby girl, and boy would that be embarrassing.

And there, frozen and lonely, I was suddenly reminded that I was completely wrong to think I was the only one awake in here.

The baby kicked for the very first time.

How could I bring a baby into this world?

I guessed that if I ever did get to sleep, I was going to have nightmares just like Deedee. And no one would reach out to comfort me, either.

DAY –5, MORNING

I'm usually the first one up. Occasionally Gripper does her freaking-me-out thing by being sat on my bed as I wake up, but six days out of seven it's me. Strange, really, because I've never been into early mornings – I'm blaming it on my hormones. Of course, these days I'm blaming everything on my hormones. But maybe it was because of my disturbed night, or because she was still sore from the injuries that I knew she had but she wouldn't tell me about, this morning Claire woke up before I did.

Her screams pierced my dreams. I blinked, not sure what was going on. I seemed to be in the wrong place. The squeaking screams coming from above, and the legs tapping soundlessly by my head. I thought I was still dreaming. It took a few seconds before I worked out what was going on.

I stumbled out of my bunk and held my arms up to Claire. She jumped into a hug, holding me tight, sobbing into my shoulder. I wasn't surprised. I'd just had the legs hitting the wall beside me; she'd had the face. Deedee next door was hanging on the other side of the glass partition, face cyanosed and swollen. The noose had been made out of blanket strips. Her eyes were wide open, and Claire must have woken to them staring straight at her. Horribly, all of Deedee's cellmates were still asleep – with the soundproofing, none of them could hear Claire screaming.

Across the glass wall was written 'YOUR NEXT SUMMERFEELD' in carmine letters. It was on Deedee's side of the wall. 'SUMMER' was slightly smudged where her dangling chest had bumped into it. There were lipstick smears across her bare breasts.

I didn't know what to do. I wanted to laugh off the threat, but it would have seemed like I was laughing at the poor dead girl. I just kept hugging Claire. Gripper and Sophia had woken up too, and were staring through the wall. I couldn't help but watch as, next door, Deedee's bunkmate Thall yawned, stretched and screamed. It was like watching a holovid with the sound off as the other two, Crow and Jevina, woke to the silent screams and added to them. Finally I managed to tear my eyes away. And as I turned I caught a flash of movement from above me.

Daglan Straklant sat cross-legged, staring through the ceiling at me. He wasn't laughing; I think I could have coped with that. He was just staring, and stroking his jaw. It was as if he were observing an interesting experiment.

I forced myself to ignore him – one of the hardest things I've ever done. I gently let go of Claire, moved over to the sink and splashed cool water from the jug over my face. That helped a bit.

I didn't know what to do with myself. I didn't want to sit on my bunk; that would be getting too close. I didn't want to sit over the other side, because then I'd be looking straight at the body. I didn't want to look up. I couldn't sit on the floor, because I'd never be able to get up again (believe me, you don't appreciate agility until you've turned into something resembling a hippo). And I wasn't entirely sure I could stay standing. What other options were there? For the moment I just concentrated on keeping my legs from wobbling, and hugged my belly.

Gripper, to my disgust but not my surprise, seemed slightly amused by it all. 'Bags me her rations this morning,' she said.

Sophia was more concerned. 'Query: are you all right?' she asked Claire and I. We both murmured something non-committal. And then she asked the real question. 'Query... did Deedee take her own life?'

'She must have,' I said stupidly. 'She's locked in her cell. Who would have killed her?' A pause. 'She had nightmares.'

Claire was squeaking in agitation. 'Benny, I'm scared! Did you see what it says?'

Oh yes. I was scared too.

But I was blaming it on my hormones.

When they finally let us out, I tried to go next door. The Aseks wouldn't let me. I tried to push past them, but they just pushed back. I ended up on my bum in the corridor. It took both Claire and Sophia to help me up, and then Claire insisted on checking me over. By the time we got to the dining hall, everyone knew what had happened.

The three of us managed to get a corner to ourselves. I don't think any of us felt much like eating, but we forced it down. Marianne and her cult cronies kept coming over to check that the 'Great Mother' was okay.

When we got back to our cell, there was a blanket-strip noose hanging over my bunk. And I knew for certain that Deedee hadn't killed herself after all.

6
Threats and Promises

DAY –5, AFTERNOON

When we returned to our cell after lunch, there was a new message on the cell wall by my bunk. 'DO YOU THINK YOUR PRITTY?'

Well, that was a puzzler. I did have a bit of an appearance crisis recently, but I'm over it now. You have to be, when your stomach looks like a basket ball. Seriously, I didn't quite know what to make of it. Nearest I could think of was those gangster-type threats: 'You wouldn't want anything to happen to that pretty face, would you?' (bad guy waves razor blade menacingly at tied up heroine). I'd have to be careful. Duh, what was I saying? I already was being careful. I'd been being careful ever since I became pregnant, doubly careful since I was stuck in prison with Daglan Straklant, and quintuply careful since Deedee had been murdered this morning seemingly as a rather over-the-top warning to me.

But as I didn't really know what this particular threat meant... They certainly didn't allow razor blades in here. No mirrors to be shattered. No cutlery in the dining room – you didn't need it with those ultra yum nutrition blocks. Though, of course, there were ways of making weapons. You don't stick several hundred ex-military in a building and expect them to forget everything they've learnt in the field.

Thall from next door cleaned off the message, and I tried to forget about it.

DAY –5, EVENING

I was on my way to the evening meal. I'd been having a bit of a nap (Claire likes me to have a nap in the afternoons), and hadn't been very with it when I woke up, so Claire and

Sophia had gone on ahead while I pulled myself together. This is before we'd accepted just how personal the threats were, of course. Later on, they wouldn't let me out of their sights. Anyway, all the cells around were deserted, everyone was already eating.

As I reached the dining room at the end of the corridor I scanned it through the walls to see where Claire and Sophia were sitting. It was then I spotted something round the corner from me, a smudge of blue in the adjoining corridor, just before the dining room door, mostly obscured by the benches between me and it. Smock-blue. Someone lying in wait for me? Was this what I'd been warned about? Someone ought to tell them that you can't ambush someone in a glass building.

I crept up to the corner, as quiet as one can be when one is the size of a house. But then I heard a whimpering sob, and I forgot about the threats and crashed straight into heroine drive, hurrying to the source of the sound as quickly as I could.

There was a woman lying in the middle of the corridor in front of me. She was about fifty, with bobbed grey hair, and she reminded me a bit of Ms Jones. In appearance only, I hasten to add, not behaviour. This woman was curled up in a ball like a denim-smocked woodlouse, arms clutched protectively over her head. I'd not seen her before – one of the new intake, I guessed.

I shuffled over to her and eventually, with much creaking and groaning (unacknowledged) managed to crouch by her side. 'What's the matter?' I asked quietly.

She lifted her head briefly, looking at me, and then her gaze slipped past me and she quickly buried her head back beneath her arms. I could hear muffled gasps coming from somewhere between her chest and her armpits.

I put an arm awkwardly across her back. 'There, there,' I said ineffectually. 'Come on, try and get up. Tell me what the problem is.'

She started up again, but only got as far as her knees

before she flung herself on to me like she was a drowning woman and I were a life jacket. I guess she may have got that impression from my considerably more ample than usual bosoms, into which her head was now burrowing. 'I'm going to fall!' came the rather indistinct cry from my breast.

Vertigo. I'd seen it before, but never this bad. Few people would lean on the outside walls, and most kept to the middle of corridors out of instinct, but there wasn't much of the whole full-on screaming phobia stuff. Thank goodness – I mean, how did you deal with it? I'd heard of two girls who had killed themselves within twenty-four hours of being incarcerated in the Glass Prison – one was claustrophobic and couldn't stand being locked in a cell; the other was agoraphobic and couldn't bear the lack of comforting non-see-through walls. You really can't please everyone.

How can you get away from heights when you're four storeys up and can see everything? 'What cell have they put you in?' I asked the woman. After several attempts, she finally told me: D8. Damn and double damn. A corner: right on the edge. That wasn't going to help much.

'It'll get better,' I told her hopelessly – and almost certainly inaccurately. 'Come on, let me help you into the dining room.' But she wouldn't move; wouldn't let go of me.

'I was all right when I couldn't see it,' she whispered. 'I kept a blanket over my head and that was okay. But they took my blanket away. They said if I didn't come and eat today…'

'Who said that?' I asked. 'The Aseks?'

A sharp half-nod.

'Bastards,' I muttered. Then, louder, 'But they're right in a way. You have to eat something. Come on, I'll help you there. You can't fall if I'm holding you.'

I shuffled her around so that I was angled between her and the outside wall. Now I came to think of it, it really did look like a very long way down…

But she'd sunk her heels in: pushing her weight to the floor, refusing to move. I didn't like to just start dragging her along by her arms, even if I could manage it with the weight I was already carrying.

'I almost made it,' I heard her say.

'Yes,' I agreed. 'Just a few more steps...'

But she wasn't having any of it. I banged on the wall of the dining room – a futile gesture, really, but someone might notice the movement. As it happened, they did. Several people looked up, then they nudged other people, and soon I had quite a large audience. I made various 'come here and help me!' gestures, but no one moved. So I pointed to Claire and Sophia, over the other side with their backs to me, and mimed for someone to get their attention. No one did. They were just enjoying the floor show.

'Wait here,' I said to the woman – like she was going to be going anywhere! – 'I'm going to fetch some friends. It'll all be all right. Trust me.'

I waddled off into the dining room. 'Thanks a lot, everyone,' I called as I opened the door. 'Really appreciate all your help. I'll be sure to call on you whenever I'm in trouble.'

Claire and Sophia turned round at that. 'Come and give us a hand, will you?' I said to them. 'This poor woman's got galloping vertigo and I can't get her to move.'

They jumped up at once. But when we got to the door, there was an Asek standing in front of it. 'Excuse me,' I said politely. It didn't move. From beside me, Claire gave a gasp. I followed her gaze towards my vertiginous friend: two Aseks had hold of her arms, and were dragging her bodily along the floor.

'Hey!' I yelled, but of course they couldn't hear me. 'Where are they taking her?' I asked the door-guarding Asek, who ignored me. I tried to push past it, but it shoved me violently backwards. Luckily Sophia managed to half-catch me and I didn't fall – and even more luckily that meant I didn't land on top of Claire, because at my current weight that might have done her serious damage – but I was pretty winded. By the time I got my breath and my bearings back, all I could see was a flash of blue and two flashes of white through the 'magic portal' – the one door that leads off our floor, situated in the corner nearest the dining room entrance.

And that was that. Never saw that woman again, never even found out her name. Never got an answer out of the Aseks as to what had happened to her (and I did try).

If you don't conform, you're stuffed.

I still ate my nutrition block. I didn't want it, but my baby did.

While I was choking down the food, a shy little thing called Primrose was going around asking if anyone had seen her spectacles. No one had. I didn't think anything of it. Personal possessions are fiercely guarded here, but that doesn't mean that nothing ever goes missing. After all, in the words of an extremely old joke, the place is full of criminals.

And I had so many other things on my mind that I didn't think of it again until bedtime, when I leaned on my bunk and felt something sharp through the blanket. I whipped the covers off. There in the middle of my bed was a small pile of glass shards.

I shut my eyes for a moment. That could have been very nasty. But… in a way, I was surprised. It seemed such a trivial thing, really, after a girl had been killed. And it didn't really square with the 'pritty' message. Now if someone had been holding a sharp chunk of spectacle lens to my cheek, that would have different…

I quickly gathered all the shards together.

The other three had come over to see what was going on. I showed them the glass. Claire and Sophia were shocked. Gripper was less so. 'Amateurish,' she said. 'Ten to one you were going to notice before you were particularly hurt.'

I ignored the lack of concern in her voice. 'Actually, I agree with you,' I said. 'I was expecting something a bit more than this.' I kept working with the pieces.

'What are you doing?' Claire asked.

I explained. 'I'm doing a jigsaw. I'm guessing that this is the remains of Primrose's spectacles, and so I'm trying to see if they're all here. That there aren't any big bits of glass still out there somewhere, that someone might try to slash me with.'

She nodded her understanding. The three of them stood beside me, trying not to block out the light, pointing out possible matches between this sliver and that one. Incredibly, unbelievably, it was actually quite fun. Shows how desperate you can get when you have to make your own entertainment. Before you know it, I'll be arranging sing-songs. 'Pack up your troubles in your old kit bag.' 'It's a long way to Tipperary.' And oh, it is a long way. I wonder if whoever wrote that song had ever envisaged it being hummed thousands of light years from Ireland.

I saw that some of the girls in the adjoining cells were looking at us curiously. I just smiled noncommittally at them.

I didn't raise my eyes to check for Straklant. I just knew he was behind this somehow. I *wouldn't* let him see he was getting to me. I *wouldn't*.

It took a painstaking hour, but in the end we came to the conclusion that the spectacle lenses were all accounted for. A few crumbs of glass might be missing, but no more than might have been overlooked when they were broken, nothing that was likely to do any damage.

'Unless they're put in your food,' Gripper said, helpfully. 'Ground-up glass sure makes a mess of your insides.'

I chose to take this seriously. 'I don't think it would be possible to doctor the food in here,' I said, 'or at least not to ensure that any one person got the dodgy stuff. No one could tell which particular food block would be dispensed to me, and there's no opportunities for sleight of hand plate swapping, as far as I can see.'

She shrugged. 'Fair enough. I'd be careful if I were you, though.' Like I said before, I am. Oh boy, I am.

I tore off a piece of blanket and swept all the glass into it. I couldn't think of what to do with it then, so I put it on the washstand to remind me to find a way to dispose of it first thing in the morning.

I glanced into the next door cell. Crow and Jevina had gone to bed. Thall was sitting on her bunk, rocking gently from side to side. Her pupils were enormous, and I suspected she'd acquired something from the Terpsechians to help her relax. Like you can relax after you've discovered your girlfriend's been hanging by the neck until she's dead...

On Earth – and almost certainly on other planets too – hanging was often used as an official punishment. It always brought the crowds. If you wanted to be a celebrity, hanging was the thing for you. And they'd take your life for any small thing: a debt, a theft, a trumped-up charge. Had Deedee committed any such crime? Who knew.

In some countries, public hangings were still going on well into the twenty-first century. It was considered an ideal method of killing, as there was no blood or guts to clear up, and you didn't need anyone particularly skilled to carry it out. Oh, the hanged man might live for minutes or hours after the drop in horrific agony, waiting to die, but that just added to the spectacle. Of course, in England, a woman due to hang could 'plead her belly' – ask for the execution to be stayed if she were pregnant – and I wondered if the murderer would allow me to plead that excuse if he came for me in the night.

That night I dreamed.

I was being taken to the gallows, my baby in my arms. We were sitting in our coffin, being carried on a cart, and the crowd was baying out for my final speech. I saw Deedee in the crowd, and oh so many other faces I recognised.

I was taken to the gibbet and the noose was placed around my neck, baby still clutched to my chest. And as though I were in a musical, I began to sing out an old English gallows ballad.

> Oh father have you brought me gold?
> Silver to pay my fee?
> Or have you come to see me hang
> On the gallows tree?

Isaac came forward and sang back:

> No I've not brought you gold
> Silver to pay your fee
> I have come to see you hang
> On the gallows tree

And I lamented:

> Oh the pricklie bush
> Grieves my heart full sore
> And if ever I get out of that pricklie bush
> I'll never get in it any more

Claire came forward and I continued

> Sister have you brought me gold?
> Silver to pay my fee?
> Or have you come to see me hang
> On the gallows tree?

And she looked cruelly at me

> No I've not brought you gold
> Silver to pay your fee
> I have come to see you hang
> On the gallows tree

And then out of the crowd came Jason, and I sang

> True love have you brought me gold?
> Silver to pay my fee?
> Or have you come to see me hang
> On the gallows tree?

Jason took the executioner aside, and began to speak to him. I strained and strained to hear what he was saying, knowing what the next verse should be, with my true love presenting me with gold and silver and taking the noose from around my neck... But I waited and waited and the words didn't come. And the crowd was yelling for my neck to snap, and as I watched Jason walked back into the crowd and the executioner came over to me and raised a hand and I was going to die I was going to feel the pain and I was going to die with my baby still in my arms...

And then, of course, I woke up. I lay shivering in the night, wondering and crying. Through the gloom, I could make out the shape of Thall next door, still swaying slightly from side to side. Whatever the Terpsechians had given her, I was guessing it was either working too well, or not well enough.

DAY –4, MORNING

When I woke up the next morning, the message by my head read: 'BETTER LUCK NEXT TIME?'

I felt cold.

I got out of bed carefully, and reached up to touch Claire's arm. My hand just hung in space for a few moments before I could bring myself to shatter her calm. Every time she breathes out, her whiskers quiver. I really love Claire. She's the closest thing I've ever had to a substitute mum. Maybe it's the prospect of becoming a mother myself that makes me need her so much.

This time it was me who needed the hug. I hushed her worried chitters as she woke, and laid my head against her shoulder. 'I'm scared,' I whispered, as quiet as I could just in case Gripper or Sophia were to wake. I don't usually say things like that. Or rather, I don't admit to the feelings. 'I've faced so many things before, but this time – this time it's not just me. How can I be responsible for another life when I haven't got the hang of my own yet?'

Claire just stroked my hair. I felt a tear begin to trickle down my nose, although I hadn't realised I was crying. Several more followed, and splashed on to Claire's fur.

I stood upright and brushed them off with a half-laughing sob. 'Sorry.'

She shook her head. Sometimes nothing needs to be said.

I helped her off the bunk, and she examined the writing on the wall. She was quite calm about it. 'You have to be very careful,' she said.

I nodded. 'I'm trying,' I said. People keep telling me to be careful! Do I need to be told? Do I seem so stupid and irresponsible? I AM BEING CAREFUL! I looked at the lipstick message again, and suddenly I couldn't stop myself laughing. '"Better luck next time"! They're talking to me about luck! After all this...' I swept my arm around, encompassing everything that had happened to me recently. The pregnancy. Jason. Prison. I just had to laugh. But it wasn't proper laughing. I think I may have been getting slightly hysterical. '"Luck be my lady tonight!"' I spluttered. I raised my hands to the ceiling and yelled: 'Lady Luck, why have you forsaken me?'

Hormones.

I sat down on my bunk and Claire sat down beside me, stroking my arm.

By now Gripper and Sophia were awake. Possibly because of the shouting, hysterics and occasional song lyrics. Sophia climbed down from her bunk. 'Query...?' she began, but then she noticed the writing.

'Query: no one else is dead?' she asked when she'd read it.

I really laughed at that. 'No! No, there's one good thing about all this. He's only killed one person so far! Unless a corpse is going to pop out of the food machine when I get my breakfast, of course!'

Sophia looked concerned. 'Fact: you are getting slightly hysterical. Under these circumstances humans require a drink of water. I will fetch one for you.'

She went over to the washstand and poured out a beakerful from the jug. As she turned away, her arm caught the blanket twist of glass shards – she yelped, and dropped the beaker. Water spilled all down her smock.

There was a sudden hiss as the fabric began to smoke.

'Oh goddess!' I cried, jumping up as best I could. Sophia was shrieking, pulling the material away from her skin. But Gripper leapt up and took charge.

'Don't pull it over your head,' she said. 'You'll get it on your face.' By this time – mere fractions of a second since the spill – the front of the smock was looking close to becoming a string vest, and little blisters were popping up on Sophia's skin. Gripper grabbed up the blanket from her bunk, held it over her hands, and ripped the dress right off. She dropped the disintegrating rag to the floor and it lay there, fizzing into nothing.

I was looking around for something, anything, that might help. There was nothing. The only thing I knew of to do with corrosives was to dilute them, and there was nothing to do that with. I ran to the door and started to bang on it in the hope that a passing Asek might notice me. I really got into a rhythm, but no one came.

'Benny! Benny!' It was Sophia, trying to get my attention. I turned.

She was obviously still shaken up, but she'd stopped yelling.

'Sophia?' I said. 'Are you all right?' A silly question, but sometimes you just can't help yourself. She glanced down at her chest, and I followed her gaze. The rubbery skin was mottled, little bubbles clustering on the surface like boiling plastic.

'Good fact: I am but minimally hurt. Very good fact: the skin of the Grel is of a type superior to that of humans, and a substance which may severely damage a human is less harmful to us.'

'Thank goodness!' I said. 'But... your skin – look at it!'

'Fact: it is surface damage only, causing pain which was extreme but momentary. The epidermis of a Grel is considerably thicker than that of a human and I can lose several layers with only minor discomfort. See, already, the corrosive substance has met its match and I can touch my

69

skin with no danger.' And it was true. The blistering had stopped, and Sophia brushed her fingers down her front. The damaged skin began to peel away, like a bad case of sunburn. The skin revealed below was bright and raw, but undamaged.

'Wow,' I said. 'That's incredible.' Then it began to sink in. 'Thank goodness! Oh goddess, what could have happened to you…'

Claire interrupted, quietly. 'What could have happened to *you*, Benny.'

'You mean if Sophia hadn't spilled it and I'd started to drink that?' I said. It didn't bear thinking about.

'No.' I looked at her. My brain wasn't functioning very fast this morning. Then it struck me.

'Almost every morning… I'm the first one up… I go over to the washstand and splash my face with water from the jug…'

'"Do you think you're pretty?"'

'So that's what he meant,' I said slowly. 'I said it didn't fit in with the glass thing. Oh goddess – Sophia, I'm so sorry! What could have happened to you, and it was intended for me!'

Gripper gave a mirthless snort. 'Sod that. She's fine. What if it had happened to someone else without rubber skin?'

She was right. If it hadn't been me, it might have been Claire. And yes, it might even have been Gripper, and much as I disliked her I wouldn't wish that on anybody. Acid-throwing had been quite in vogue in the early years of the twentieth century, I'd discovered during my studies – vitriol for choice. A double helping of pain and disfigurement. Horrific. Nice to know that human nature hasn't changed over the last seven hundred years.

I waddled back to my bunk and took off the blanket, giving it to Sophia to wrap round herself. She took it gratefully. Gripper even indicated space on the bottom bunk for her to sit – now that was a first. 'You can get a new smock when the Aseks come round,' I said. 'They can't argue that you need one.' We're only allowed a new smock when an Asek judges that our current one is unwearable. (And unfortunately for me, smell is not acceptable grounds for a replacement. Damn their non-nasality!)

But Sophia's mind didn't seem to be on her wardrobe. 'Query: who is "he"?' she asked me.

I was puzzled. 'I'm sorry?'

'Fact: you stated "so that's what he meant" in regard to the threats you have received. Earlier you stated "He's only killed one person so far". My inference is that you are referring to the individual Straklant for whose incarceration you were responsible, but logically this makes no sense: no male is permitted to enter this floor.'

'But I know it's him!' I said, possibly a little louder than was strictly necessary. 'Who else would want to hurt me this much?'

'Fact: the Wolf was unfriendly to you.'

I shook my head. 'No, that doesn't make sense. Whatever she thinks about me, she wouldn't risk harming this.' I patted my stomach. 'It's Straklant.'

'Why would Straklant kill Deedee, though?' asked Claire. 'Surely no one would kill a person just to frighten someone else?'

'You've never met a member of the Fifth Axis security force before, have you Claire?' I said, darting a bit of an evil look at Gripper. 'To them, a good reason for killing someone would be "looking at them in a funny way" or "blocking their sunlight". They don't have to think up reasons to kill people, they have to think up reasons to keep them alive. Oh, perhaps Deedee had annoyed him in some way – that might be why he picked her – or he might have done eeny-meeny-miny-mo on the people in the cells next to ours and she just happened to be "mo", poor thing.'

Sophia's tentacles wobbled. 'Reluctant restatement: the killing could not have been done by Straklant. He could not get to this floor from his own.'

'But it has to have been... wait!' That was it! 'There must

be some way of getting from floor to floor that we don't know about!' I cried. 'And if there is... we might be able to get out of here! We might be able to get a message out about the Axis's big conference!'

There was a choke from Gripper. 'How the hell do you know about *that*?' she yelled. And then she went very quiet. Her eyes opened wide as she realised what she'd done.

'Oh shit,' I said. 'You're still one of them, aren't you.'

7
My Enemy's Enemy...

It turned out to be a more civilised conversation than we had any right to expect. Gripper obviously realised that there was no way she could cover up her monumental slip up – even if she'd been able to think up a convincing cover story, her eyes had given her away immediately. So she told us, plainly and simply, what she claimed to be the truth. I'm not saying I believe it all, but it does, at least, make a vague kind of sense.

The Fifth Axis knew all about this Mothering Cult, as she called it. They knew about the prophecy, and they knew that the current members of the cult believed it to refer to the overthrowing of the Axis forces on Deirbhile. But they didn't mind the cult. It was almost universal on Deirbhile, and they found it easier to put up with it and have servile locals to do their bidding than kill them all and have to bring in servitors from elsewhere.

They knew that the cult thought that my baby was the one. They knew the cult were having me brought to Deirbhile. 'Did they know how?' I interrupted. But it seemed that their knowledge didn't spread that far. Or if it did, Gripper didn't share it. She thought it was probably some other 'liberated' Axis device that the cult had put on my ship. 'But how did they get it on it?' I said. 'They would have had to have had someone on the Braxiatel Collection at the time I decided to leave!' But Gripper really didn't know.

They could have killed me. They could have shot down my ship, or bashed me over the head with a blunt instrument when we landed. They chose not to. They were – well, cunning. Luckily for me, I suppose. They let us land – actually crash, of course, but I wasn't going to quibble at this late stage – but made sure that they, and not the cult, were the first on the scene. They took me to the Glass Prison, to the floor which housed the greatest number of influential cultists. They put an Axis agent in my cell to keep an eye on me. When they judged the time was right, they were going to pull in a load more cult leaders, to be witnesses. Unfortunately they had to move the timetable forward a couple of days unexpectedly because news of the operation was being leaked, but...

'Hang on a minute here,' I interrupted again. 'When "the time was right" for what? What timetable? Are you talking about this military "operation"?'

Gripper raised an eyebrow. 'I may have been hired to protect you. I may have given away some information I shouldn't have. But you know what? We still don't like each other and I'm not going to start giving you confidential details of our forces plans.'

'Yeah, yeah, yeah,' I said. 'So, when "the time was right" for what?'

'Well, when you're due to give birth, obviously,' Gripper said.

Claire squeaked. 'You mean they think Benny's going to give birth soon?' she said.

Gripper shrugged. 'That's what they told me. I'm no scientist. They estimate it will take place this Saturday.'

Saturday? *This* Saturday? *Four days from now?* I couldn't think of anything to say.

'But how have they calculated it?' Claire asked. 'We were unable to find any records of human-Killoran matings...'

'Fact,' began Sophia, 'there are no fewer than three human-Killoran dual parentages recorded on –' But I waved her down. I had now thought of something to say.

'*Four... days...*' I said, blankly.

'That's what they say.'

Four days. If Gripper were to be believed, there were less than 96 hours before I became a mother.

'Four days,' I said again. It really was the only thing that popped into my head.

I was only vaguely aware of Sophia continuing the

conversation with Gripper.

'Query: why did the hostile forces of the Fifth Axis wish to keep Benny alive? Additional query: why did they wish cultists present at the time of childbirth?'

And Gripper explained. Really, why did everything have to be so *complicated* around the Fifth Axis? They wanted me alive, she said, because an alive nobody is less trouble than a dead martyr. They wanted the child of the prophecy to be born, and born under the control of the Fifth Axis. They wanted the cult leaders to witness the birth, and declare the child to be their saviour, no question of a mistake: a prophecy part-fulfilled. And then the cultists would be there, in a Fifth Axis prison, with their saviour, and see it was no such thing. The Axis would still be in charge. Nothing would be happening. The prophecy was, to put it frankly, bollocks. And then, they believed, the cult would collapse, and with it all resistance to the Axis forces on Deirbhile.

It made sense, of a sort, I supposed. Although I think they underestimate the human capacity for hope.

'And now we've got that out of the way,' Gripper said, 'perhaps we can devote some energy to working out who's trying to kill you. So I can deal with them.' She smiled. 'After all, we do want you alive. At least until Saturday.'

I didn't smile back. I was still thinking: four days...? But I said, 'I know who's trying to kill me. And he'll be sitting right up there now, watching us.'

Gripper looked up, towards Straklant's cell. 'There's no one watching us,' she said. 'There's no one there at all. Everyone's gone to breakfast.'

And do you know what? She was right. It must have been the first time ever that we'd not noticed the doors being released. We agreed to discuss the matter further after we'd eaten.

To be honest, I'd probably have agreed to anything right then. I think I was a bit in shock. Claire had to virtually lead me to the dining room, her little paw stretched up to my numb hand. All of me was numb right now. 'It'll be all right,' she whispered.

'It'll be all right,' I echoed under my breath. I didn't sound at all convincing. 'But... so many things...'

Sophia, blanket clutched tightly around her, shook her head compassionately. 'As humans say: "It never rains, but it pours",' she said. 'This means that once bad things come along, more bad things will come along too, and does not relate directly to precipitation, as facts show that in actuality fifty-seven per cent of rain could in no way be described as a "pour", giving the lie to the...'

I switched off at that point. But I think I appreciated the sentiment.

Suddenly I realised that Sophia had stopped discussing the veracity of popular sayings. We'd reached the dining room, and she'd halted in the doorway to talk to one of the Aseks, explaining about her smock.

The Asek indicated for her to drop the blanket. She shook her head, telling it that she wasn't wearing the old smock underneath. It held out a hand for the old smock – they had to inspect it so they could decide if she deserved a new one.

'It disintegrated!' I chimed in. 'There's nothing left of it.'

The Asek indicated it didn't believe me. It gestured again for Sophia to lose the blanket. I knew she didn't want to. Sophia wasn't the shiest of us – Grel don't have enough imagination for that – but by now most of D floor were watching us over their breakfasts. Like I say, you get entertainment where you can.

'Bad fact: my clothing has been destroyed by acid! I am wearing only this blanket!' Sophia cried as the Asek looked her up and down with its expressionless eyes.

It reached forward and grabbed the blanket from her. Some of the girls in the dining room cheered.

Sophia's raw skin grew even brighter as a blush crept all over. She asked for the blanket back, but the Asek turned and handed it to a colleague.

'She doesn't have a smock!' I yelled at its back. 'Don't you understand?'

It ignored me. I was getting mad, and Sophia seemed

frozen to the spot with embarrassment.

Well, sod the Aseks, and sod Straklant, and sod my dignity. I pulled my own giant-sized smock over my head and handed it to Sophia. 'Here,' I said. 'Put it on.'

My tone did not allow for disagreement. Wordlessly, she took the dress from me.

There was more cheering from the girls in the dining room as I stood starkers in the doorway, hands firmly on hips, enormous belly thrust out proudly, and defiant look in my eyes. 'Right, everyone, breakfast?' I said, beginning to walk through into the room. Claire was trotting beside me, eyes wide.

But the first Asek had turned back to us. It grabbed my smock from Sophia before she'd got it half way to her waist, dragged it back over her head, and shoved it back towards me.

'No,' I said, evenly, 'I've given it to my friend Sophia, because you wouldn't let her have a new one.'

It kept pushing the thing at me insistently. And so I took it. I took the blue material in both hands, ripped it neck to hem, and handed it back to the Asek. There were screams of joy and encouragement from the girls in the hall. 'My smock is damaged,' I said. 'I need a new one.'

DAY –4, MORNING/AFTERNOON/EVENING

Mister Crofton has a greenhouse on the Braxiatel Collection. It's quite small, although Brax would have provided a much bigger one if Mister Crofton had asked for it. The left-hand side is full of fruit and vegetables, and the right-hand side is full of flowers. There are varieties from all over the galaxy and beyond – sweet melons and tomatoes and cucumbers bigger than your arm, and blooms of every colour, from infrared-hot-pokers to ultraviolets. But there's a central pathway between the fruit and flowers where the sunshine is unrestricted. It's one of Wolsey's favourite spots. My cat, macho tom though he may be, is a sucker for sunlight. He'll lay stretched out, creating the biggest possible surface area for the rays to warm, and not move until the sun goes in, or until Mister Crofton disturbs his bliss with an unpleasant shower from a watering can. Sometimes, if the weather is particularly nice, he'll even forget to come in for tea. If you have a cat, you'll realise just how incredible that is.

I am pretending I am a cat. If I were Wolsey, I tell myself, I would love this.

I am unconvinced.

I am on A floor of the Glass Prison. They are not torturing me. They are just teaching me a lesson.

Since we arrived in the Glass Prison, there haven't been any deaths from sunstroke on D floor. At least we can thank the so-called 'civilised' Fifth Axis that water isn't rationed, recovered and chemically-tainted though it may be; now that medically-trained Claire has shown people what to do the danger is even less, and anyway the glass problem isn't as bad as you might think. Deirbhile is not known for its summer holiday weather, and by the time you get to our floor there are so many things in the way – people, bunks, tables and so on – that the sunlight doesn't hit you that hard on ordinary days. The higher you get, the worse it is, of course – on the sunniest days, rumours begin to fly about the number of people who've collapsed up on K floor. You'd think the albino-esque Aseks would suffer too, but no such luck – they seem to have as much feeling as plastic.

If they had any feeling at all, they wouldn't – couldn't – have put me here.

There is nothing between me and the sun, nothing except layer after layer of glass. I imagine a yellow crayoned circle in the sky, and the yellow beams shooting out of it get wider and wider and deeper and deeper until they reach me and fill the page. I am covered in yellow, naked in the sun.

I know all about sunstroke. It's a very real danger on expeditions on most worlds. You're digging hard all day, out in the open, so excited by your finds you've not even thought to stop and take a drink, your hat's fallen off and you find you're getting dizzier and dizzier…

It's one of the first things I taught my students. Common sense and discipline, I'd say. You know the mad old professors of fiction, so caught up in their work that they don't notice what's going on around them? Don't be like that. And they'd nod, and vow to be sensible always.

First you get dizzy, then you get sick. Your heads pounds and you can't move. You stop sweating. Your pulse races. You lose consciousness. You die.

I'm already dizzy and sick.

Help is so close at hand. Is it deliberate? Is it designed to cause extra suffering? Not far away – but not near enough to cast a shadow – is the room where they keep our confiscated belongings. And there, only metres away, a little round ball is bobbing up and down, lights blinking on its surface. I know, even though I can't hear, that Joseph is trying to speak to me. His visual recognition circuits are very powerful; he knows I'm here. He's trying to warn me that I'm in danger. He's being the little fusspot who nags me to remember my hat and fill my flask with fresh water. He knows the sun can kill.

Your head pounds, and you can't move.

Even if you survive, there might be brain damage.

Even if you survive, there might be *baby* damage.

I talk to my baby, tell it not to worry. Everything will be all right. Neither of us are alone, and we never will be. I tell it that I love it. Like St Peter after the cock had crowed thrice, I will never deny my baby again. He is mine.

Sophia had been impressed with the naming of St Peter; it had been one of the tales she'd told me. His name was Simon, but when he'd embraced Christianity, Jesus, the Christian messiah, had named him Peter – our translation – meaning 'rock'. 'I will build my church on this rock,' he allegedly said.

If St Peter really was guarding the gates to heaven, I'd meet him soon enough and be able to ask him if that was true.

You stop sweating.

Your pulse races.
You lose consciousness.
You die.
I'm walking on sunshine. And it don't feel good.

A cooling breeze is wafting over me. Rain begins to fall, and it's wonderful. Then I open my eyes and see that Sophia is fanning me with a blanket, and Claire is pouring water over me. Jug after jug of cold water. She bathes my forehead and my wrists. I sense her little paws running over my stomach. When I am finally cool, she tells me that everything will be all right.

When I recover, I decide not to talk about it. The only thing I ask is if my baby is okay. Claire says yes, and I stop her saying any more. We have other things to think about now.

8
The Curious Case of the Countless Killers

Other things to think about.

Sophia has a new smock, and I have a new smock. Gripper and I both have new blankets. Gripper has disposed of the glass shards – I don't know how and I didn't ask. If she was the one wanting to hurt me I'd be dead soon enough, glass or no glass.

She wasn't the one wanting to hurt me, I was fairly sure of that. But we still made an uncomfortable alliance.

'Let me go through the facts as I understand them,' Gripper began when the four of us had sat down together after breakfast. Sophia let out a little eep of excitement at the word 'facts'.

'Someone has killed the girl Deedee. A person, presumably the same one, has been writing threatening messages directed at Bernice, and made several attempts to injure, although probably not kill, her.'

'Straklant,' I said. 'Killing me quickly wouldn't be punishment enough. He wants me to suffer first.'

Gripper ignored me. 'I can tell you that this is not the work of the Fifth Axis,' she said. 'Could it be the work of the Mothering Cult?'

Claire jumped in there. 'No. They might want to punish Benny for not believing in their prophecy, but they *do* believe in it, so wouldn't do anything that could cause harm to the baby, even indirectly.'

'From my observations, Bernice has made no enemies since entering the prison,' Gripper continued. 'It was actually quite a surprise to me. From my briefing I had

81

understood her to be more of a… trouble maker.'

'Everyone has to calm down sometime,' I said. There was a pause. 'Look, I'm telling you it's Straklant!'

Gripper shook her head. 'I can guarantee that there is no way at all that he could have come from E down here. Not only is there only the one possible connection between the two floors, but *any* unauthorised interfloor activity would have triggered numerous alarms.'

'But –' I began.

'*Nevertheless*,' she said, 'I agree that he is the most likely candidate. But he has not carried out the acts himself. He has an ally on this floor.'

An ally. I suppose I had known that really. But I was obsessed. Obsession, by Bernice Summerfield. And of course my brain really wasn't working well at the moment. Damn these hormones!

'And as the murder of Deedee and the composition of two of the messages took place overnight in a locked room, it's obviously one of her cell mates. The only question is, which one?'

Yes, all right, I suppose I'd known that too. In fact, I'd said it straight away. She was locked in her cell – who would have killed her but herself? I'd said, knowing that there were three other candidates still living and breathing right on hand. But all three of Deedee's cellmates had seemed so shocked at her death – and whoever it was must have taken some almighty risks to do it without the others noticing - and I just hadn't wanted to believe it was someone so close. Someone I'd chatted to, someone I regularly waved at through the walls. So I'd suppressed it. Focused on Straklant. Refused to suspect anyone else.

Of course, no one else had pointed out the obvious either. So it wasn't just me.

'You're right,' said Claire. 'I've been keeping an eye on all three of them, but I haven't seen anything suspicious.

Oh. I turned to Claire. 'You'd already worked this out?'

She looked bashful. 'Well, it did seem the most likely thing. If Deedee didn't kill herself…'

Gripper's tentacles were flubbering. 'Not you too?' I said, pained. 'So I really am Ms Stupid Repression 2600, then.'

'Fact: I had made certain inferences. But in the absence of proof, I had decided to keep such to myself until I had found more facts! Also, I was acting in the manner advocated by humans, as they say "If you can't say anything nice, don't say anything at all."'

'That's not quite what it...' I began, but didn't have the will to go on.

Gripper was smiling. 'Oh, I think we should be able to find more facts easily enough.'

'Oh yeah?' I said, defensively. Okay, so they were trying work out how to save my life here, but I didn't have to be gracious about it. 'How exactly?'

'The second of the messages was left during the lunch period. The jug was filled with acid at some point before evening lock-in.'

'So?'

'So we're in a see-through building. Someone will have spotted something.'

Oh. Yeah.

Am I loosing it? Am I wandering around in a hormone-induced dopey haze? Or was I always this clueless? Nah, can't be that. You don't manage to stay alive this long when you're in the adventuring/world-saving business (however unintentionally) without a bit of savvy. And believe it or not – and I wouldn't blame you for 'not', but trust me for the moment – I've often been commended for my intelligence and cool-headedness. And I *was* both. I *know* I was. When I think back to some of the things I've done – have had to do...

Benny, infiltrate this top-secret organisation. No problem!

Benny, you're posing as a high-ranking government official. Whatever you say!

Benny, the fate of the whole planet rests on you making the right decision. Don't sweat it!

I think I just got too suspicious. That sounds ridiculous

coming from someone who's being Oblivious Girl, but the thing is I was *too* cynical. Especially after Jason. He ripped my heart right out, the git. And I never did find closure. Divorce, desertion, other disastrous 'relationships', reconciliation (of a sort), more desertion, disaster and reconciliation – in fact, almost ad infinitum – with a final strange demon dimension desertion thing. Even now, now I know he's alive and all that stuff, and we're not exactly getting on like a house on fire (that was a difficult saying for Sophia to understand. Took me a while to explain why it's a *good* thing, even if it does refer to utter destruction of property in a terrifying way, because, frankly, I don't think it makes sense in the slightest either) – well, even now I don't understand what we've got there, because I refuse to admit there is a 'we', whilst at the same time clinging to the idea like a life raft in a sea of utter relationship crappiness.

So I had this major Jason betrayal to deal with, and this whole host of little betrayals alongside. It wears you down. I thought everyone was out to use me, probably because they were. I was being set up as the Fall Girl. I was made to think people liked me when they just wanted something (and not *that* sort of something, either).

When you're a little girl, you're brought up to think that men are only after one thing. It comes as quite a shock to find out that this is a blatant lie, and they're actually after a lot of things, such as Money; Someone to Take the Blame; Priceless Artefacts that Only You Know How to Find; Other Men; a Secret of the Universe to which You Hold the Key; to Kill You. It really would make a lovely change to find someone who just wanted to sleep with me. Or, most of the time pre-pregnancy, someone who wanted to sleep with me, full stop.

I've always been... naturally cynical, shall we say. But above that, I'd had a belief in the basic goodness of people. And then I lost it. I realised that I could count the people I trusted on the thumbs of my hands (and one of those people was a cat). I suspected everyone. I stopped taking anything on trust. And it was one of the most painful periods of my life. So I think I switched off. Stopped over-analysing – stopped analysing at all. Told myself to take everyone at face value. If I assumed they were nice, they would *be* nice.

Yeah, yeah, that was a bit stupid. Daglan Straklant taught me that – that's Kolonel Daglan Straklant of the Fifth Axis Security Elite, and not, as I was led to believe, Daglan Straklant of the nice bit of the Fifth Axis who were just a bit worried about art treasures, and wouldn't keep killing people as soon as my back was turned, oh no.

I'm going to start suspecting everyone again now.

Starting with Thall, Crow and Jevina from next door. At least one of whom had tried to give me an acid face wash.

Did I want to tip off my hand? Did I want to confront them directly, let whoever it was know I knew; try to 'persuade' them to confess?

No, I decided, I didn't. We'd do the detective bit first. Find some evidence.

What did I know about them?

Thall is a bit of a grunt. She's mixed species, part of which is human but I'm not sure about the rest of it. Something with scales, any way. She and Deedee had been pretty close, though – in fact, very close; take this from someone who was only a transparent wall away from their bunk. Deedee was a sweet, pretty thing, and Thall was her big bad protectoress. That's how it had seemed, anyway. I didn't know what she was in for, but I was guessing violence of some sort. The sneakiness involved in the attacks didn't seem to fit her, and although I could see her attacking Deedee in a jealous rage, I couldn't see her being so coldly calculating, or using it as part of a way to get to me. I also couldn't see her working for Straklant. But, with my new-found suspicious hat on, I could also imagine that the whole thing was an act: she didn't care for Deedee, she was pretending to be brash and loud so no one would think of her as the sneaky sort. She could be a Fifth Axis groupie for all we knew. Straklant might have promised her endless riches or power or freedom.

(And that was something I really had to work on. What could Straklant possibly be bargaining with, given that he had no authority any more, and couldn't pass stuff between floors? By the way, in case you're trying to work out how Straklant would have communicated with someone on another floor, plenty of sign language and lip reading (and reading of various other body parts) goes on across the borders. You get adept at non-verbal communication pretty quickly in this place.)

So, Thall: a possibility, assuming she's a damn fine actress.

Next: Crow. Not her real name. Human, beaky nose and lank black hair. Prison types tend to be not over-imaginative in their nick names. Now there was someone who, going by appearances, registered pretty high on the sneakometer. But, one should never judge by appearance, *bad* Benny. Bit of a loner. Tended to sit by herself at meals – well, obviously not *literally* by herself, there weren't enough benches, but she didn't hang out with a group, and didn't seem to care. Didn't seem to want company. If you did speak to her, you got the impression she was laughing at you inside. Superiority complex, maybe? She *seems* the sort who'd agree to do this stuff just because she felt like it, not because Straklant was offering some incredible reward.

A definite possibility.

Which leaves: Jevina. A pretty young thing: fluffy hair in that mauve shade, and big blue eyes. Least likely suspect if you go by appearances: looks like she wouldn't say boo to a goose. The rumour mill says she spurned a Fifth Axis officer and he got her sent here on trumped-up charges. If true, implies no love lost between her and the Axis – so would she work for Straklant? *But*, also implies some strength of character, if she was capable of standing up to some guy in authority – belying her 'no goose booing' appearance. Could it all be a fake? Another cause for suspicion – although not a cultist (as far as I know), she is close friends with Primrose, the girl whose glasses were stolen.

So, opportunity for acquiring weapon: good.

Still no idea where *any* of them could have got acid from

– we're working on that.

My gut feeling was that it was Jevina, though. But I think that's because I really think it's Crow, and my gut feeling is not to trust my instincts at the moment.

DAY –3, AFTERNOON

We four cell mates grabbed a bench at lunchtime and glared at anyone who tried to join us.

'Anyone found anything?' I asked.

Claire cleared her throat. 'I talked to the girls in 18 and 27,' (they're the two other cells sharing walls with next door) 'but they couldn't tell me much. No one was awake during the night when Deedee was killed. But then I spoke to Miroxl in 28' (the cell in front of ours) 'and she says she saw a human in our cell yesterday who wasn't Benny or Gripper. But she's not very good at telling you apart. I asked if it were one of the ones from 19, but she wasn't sure – she said possibly. She couldn't even tell me if they had dark or light hair.'

'Still, it's something,' I said. 'That could let Thall out; she's not human.'

Claire wrinkled her nose. 'But she doesn't look that different, except for the scales. For people who aren't that clear on humans, she could pass.'

I nodded. She was probably right. 'Anyone else?'

Sophia spoke. 'Fact: Jevina was with Primrose in her cell shortly before she noticed her ocular improvement device was missing. Inference: it is possible that Jevina took this.'

'Good one, Sophia,' I said. 'I'm inclining towards Jevina myself. It's nowhere near enough, though.'

'How about this, then?' said Gripper. She pulled a small plastic tube from her pocket, and pulled the top off. Red. A lipstick. 'Found it under Jevina's mattress.'

'Which proves it's not her,' I sighed. 'Everyone knows that you never keep the evidence yourself.'

'But lipstick,' said Claire. 'That's worth a lot. Maybe she couldn't bring herself to get rid of it.'

I capitulated. 'Yes, I suppose that's possible. Though I never saw her wear lipstick. But we're still not getting anywhere.'

'Idea: the safest time to enter our cell unobserved would be during meal times, as D20 is not in direct line of sight from the dining room. Specifically: breakfast yesterday for the noose; lunch yesterday for the further message; evening meal for the broken glass and the corrosive substance substitution. Idea: discover if anyone was absent for a substantial amount of those times.'

I thought about it. The logic was fine, as far as it went. But there were way over a hundred prisoners, and they didn't all come for their meals on the dot. Still, it was a possible line of enquiry. Better than a kick in the teeth, as they say.

'Additional idea: question them, make them think you suspect someone else and let them talk to you. For, as human's say: "Give a man enough rope and he will ha–"'... oh.'

Thanks for that, Sophia. Maybe not. There was an embarrassed pause, which I decided I'd better break. 'If we could just find out where the acid came from…' I said. 'If we knew that, I'm sure we'd know whodunit.'

'Suggestion: why not ask the Wolf?' said Sophia. 'If there is a source, she may know it.'

'Yes, I think I will,' I said. It was the closest thing to a plan we'd come up with. 'But this time… on my terms.'

We were locked in as usual all afternoon, so I wasn't able to go to see the Wolf straight away. There wasn't an awful lot we could do constructively, or not to do with finding the killer/would-be killer anyway. I lay on the floor practising breathing and relaxation techniques with Claire. Just in case Gripper was right and I only had until Saturday. One of the guys in the cell above was doing press-ups. He grinned at me every time his nose touched the ceiling. One of my few blessings to count: the guys directly up there seemed reasonable sorts. Didn't leer or moon at you through the ceiling the way some of them did. This one even gave me a thumbs up when I managed a particularly challenging breath.

My thoughts drifted to the birthing pool that Brax had been going to have built for me. To think, I'd been arguing about exactly how I was going to give birth. Now I'd give anything just to have a more comfortable mattress to lie on.

Claire says she's going to talk to the Aseks. She thinks they might let me out to go to a hospital. I think the chances of that happening are about the same as me being crowned Ms Universe 2600, especially given what Gripper's told us, but I'm not going to stop her. After all, anything's possible. Some of the Ms Universe judges might favour the heavily-pregnant aging-professor look.

I was keeping my eyes averted from cell D19 and its residents. But Gripper was sitting on the edge of her bunk, staring straight in. Doing that disconcerting thing she does so well. I think it'll put off whoever it is doing all this. I hope.

'Of course,' said Gripper cheerfully, as she gazed next door-wards, 'all three of them could be in it together.'

Claire squeaked, and I glared at Gripper. 'You should know all about killers,' I said. 'Do assassins usually work in packs?'

She shrugged.

'It is most unlikely,' Sophia said. 'For it is a fact that murderers usually exercise their plans alone: as humans say, "Too many cooks spoils the broth".' Then she paused, and looked troubled. 'But additional and contradictory fact: "Many hands make light work".' Her facial tentacles wobbled in the way I'd come to learn indicated she was processing data. 'Assimilation of data: although the many hands of too many cooks may make the making of the broth light work, their presence will unfortunately cause the easily-made broth to spoil. Conclusion: a lighter work load does not guarantee good results.'

'Wow,' I said. 'When we get out of here, have you ever considered a job making fortune cookies, Sophia?'

Of course, then I had to spend the rest of the afternoon explaining fortune cookies, and answering all Sophia's queries which branched off from that. We were on to the pottery of the Ming dynasty of Old Earth by teatime. Teatime! How absurd that I should use a word like that, resonant with images of bone china and lace doilies; iced fairy cakes, thin-cut cucumber sandwiches and civilised conversation, to describe the part of the day when we're herded into a deafening cattle-pen full of plastic benches, all criminals together, and presented with an insufficient nutrition block and a beaker of recycled water.

I could murder a cucumber sandwich right now.

Note to self: stop using the word 'murder' in everyday contexts.

DAY −3, EVENING

I went to see the Wolf after the evening meal. Claire insisted on coming with me. I think she doesn't want me out there alone just in case I suddenly start to give birth in the middle of a corridor. Or in case someone tries to kill me, of course.

The Wolf's in D1 − legend has it that she was the first prisoner on the floor. There was a cultist stationed in the corridor outside her cell. 'What's your business with the Wolf?' she asked me.

'It's private,' I said.

'I'm sorry, if she's not expecting you...'

I waved to the Wolf through the cell wall and rolled my eyes. 'No, I'm the one who's sorry. You'll never believe this, but for one crazy moment I thought I was visiting a fellow prison inmate, not making an appointment to see the president of Earth. What am I like, huh?'

The cultist didn't say anything.

'Look, cult-girl, I am the Great Mother, about to give birth to your prophesied saviour child, and let me tell you there are lots of other cults out there who'd be very interested in having a saviour child of their very own if you don't want it. And I'll assume you don't want it if your leader can't even be bothered to see me...'

There was a call from inside the cell. 'Let them in, Finny.'

I swept past the girl. 'No refreshments, thank you,' I called back over my shoulder. 'Although you might fetch me an extra cushion.'

The Wolf inclined her head to us. 'Bernice, Claire.'

'Hey, Wolfy,' I said, recklessly, plonking myself down on a bunk. 'Nice of you to see us without an appointment. I realise your social calendar must be pretty hectic this time of year, what with all that kidnapping people, planning to steal their babies, that sort of thing.'

'Can I help you, Bernice?' she said, coolly.

I opened my mouth for another withering comment, but Claire got in first. 'Someone's trying to kill Benny!' she squeaked. 'And they'll hurt the baby too!'

That made Wolf-woman sit up. 'No harm is going to come to this baby,' she said, eyes narrowed into slits. 'My girls are already on to it.'

'Oh, are they now? And what have they discovered?' I asked.

'We thought if you knew where the acid came from, we'd be able to find out if it's Jevina or Crow,' Claire put in. I attempted to nudge her to keep quiet, but my elbow didn't quite reach. She managed to say, 'Benny thinks it's probably Jevina,' before I kicked her on the ankle. Okay, so it looked like the Wolf already knew what was going on – unsurprisingly. But we were here to get information, not give it. And I still really didn't know if I thought it was Jevina or not.

At which point fate intervened: Grel-shaped fate, to be precise. Sophia seemed to be having a problem getting past the cultist outside, though, until I pointed her out to the Wolf. 'Benny!' she cried, as she ran in, 'New Fact! New Fact!' I motioned for her to sit down next to me, and asked what the matter was.

'New fact! Sara in D21 observed Jevina the human in our cell – bending over your bunk! Inescapable inference: it was she who placed the broken glass pieces in your bedding!'

Claire was jumping up and down, her paws bunched into tiny fists. 'I'm gonna get her! I'm gonna get her!' she squealed.

'Whoa!' I said, trying to calm her down. 'Sara isn't the brightest candle in the chandelier. Is she quite sure about this?'

'She came and told Gripper,' Sophia said. 'Gripper told me to find you. She thought you'd want to know straight away.'

Maybe it was my recent dose of suspicion, but I couldn't believe it was this easy. 'Thanks,' I said. 'I'm going to have to think about this, though.'

The Wolf smiled at me. 'No need for you to have to think about anything at all. It's not good for an expectant mother to worry. Just go and rest and let me sort this out for you.'

'I don't think so,' I said. 'It's me that's being threatened here, remember. It's up to me how I deal with it.'

She was still smiling. 'No harm is going to come to you while you are carrying our child. Believe me.'

I had a lot of things I wanted to say to that. But it was Claire's turn to kick me on the ankle. I decided just getting out of there without actually having discovered anything was the better part of valour. The three of us left.

'Well, that was a disaster,' I said, back in our cell.

'Maybe not,' Claire said. 'You might not like the cult, but they'll definitely do anything they can to protect you.'

'For now,' I said, ungraciously.

'So they'll sort out Jevina…'

'Hang on a minute,' I said. 'We don't know for sure it's Jevina. The evidence is so shallow it can hardly even be called circumstantial.'

'Question: you are feeling sympathy for your attacker?' asked Sophia.

'No! Quite frankly, I don't care what motivation someone may have, there is *never* a good reason to try to hurt me. But I'm not going off half-cocked. If Jevina definitely is my attacker she won't get any sympathy. But I want it proved first. Did I not mention to you the human adage: "Innocent till proven guilty"? Look, can we talk about something else?'

'What do you want to talk about?' Claire asked.

'Human nomenclature!' Sophia cried, eagerly. 'That is always a most diverting subject of discussion; also it is extremely relevant at this time!'

I shrugged. 'All right. It's not like I've made my mind up yet. Give us some suggestions, Sophia.'

'Query: what qualities are you hopeful of this child possessing?' she said. Well, that was a question and a half. I mean, I couldn't think of a single positive quality I didn't want it to have, or a single negative quality that I wasn't hoping it would miss out on.

'Oooh, kindness, generosity, bravery, intelligence, empathy, wisdom, strength, a cute nose...' I began. I sounded like Sleeping Beauty's fairy godmothers, wishing her all the nice things in the world. Before a prick spoiled it all.

'Suggestion: the virtue "strength" is represented by the human name "Andrew" or "Andreas", further meaning "warrior",' Sophia began.

'Stop right there,' I told her. 'I've spent my life fighting. My child is not going to be a warrior if I can help it. I see him or her more as a... a healer.'

'Ah,' said Sophia. 'There is a name meaning healer, it is "Jason".'

I choked. 'I am not calling my child Jason! That is in all probability number one on my list of things I am not going to inflict on this baby, even edging out dressing it in frilly pink dresses and making it eat pureed broccoli.'

Claire said: 'I think you'd better suggest some more names quickly, Sophia. How about... ones that reflect the mothers feelings towards the child.'

'Horror, dread, anticipation of severe pain...'

'Hmmm... suggestion: the human name "Pryderi" means "anxiety".'

'She wasn't being serious, Sophia.'

'Says who, Claire?'

'Nice things, like "love" or "happiness" please, Sophia,' said Claire, placatingly.

'Ah. Further suggestions: "David" meaning "beloved", "Felicity" meaning "felicity"...'

'That's more like it. More please.'

Friends. They can make you forget your problems. At least for a while.

9
Dreams of Violence

I hated her. I really hated her. I wanted to punch and slap and kick her, pull her hair and scream in her face. She had killed someone – not really a friend, but someone who might have become one. She had hurt people I cared about. She had tried to hurt me.

She had tried to hurt my baby.

I could watch people laying into her with a sneer on my face, not turning a hair.

I like to think of myself as a good person. Holding out a hand to the enemy who's hanging off a cliff. Not stabbing the bad guy when he's dropped his sword. That sort of thing. Not standing by while someone's torn limb from limb.

Torn limb from limb. That's one of those phrases that is considerably overused, and rarely meant literally. Have you ever thought about what it's really saying? Try and imagine it, now multiply the horror in your head by ten and you still won't know what it's like to watch it happening. Mind you, it wasn't the watching that was the worst bit; it was the sound. You know that sickening ripping, snapping sound when someone's jointing poultry or something? Tearing off a human arm makes the same sort of noise, only louder. The sound creeps up, under the screaming, and then just for the single crack it rises above it. Then as the ripping dies down the volume of the screams falls too, because the person is so consumed with the pain they don't have any energy left for screaming. And, of course, because they're going to be dead soon.

Okay, this is how it actually happened. I'm going to try to be quite clinical about it.

I hadn't slept very well. The baby was obviously not

sleeping either, instead choosing to stomp around my womb. Maybe it was going to be an explorer when it grew up. Or perhaps a champion trampolinist, as it was also taking the opportunity to bounce on my bladder, and I was needing to go to the loo what felt like every other minute. It's amazing how quickly you learn to find a toilet in the dark. After the first couple of times I didn't bang my shins once. The worst bit is having to keep heaving yourself off the bed in the first place. Thank goodness Claire had insisted on my having the bottom bunk.

However calm you are before bedtime, everything comes back to haunt you in the middle of the night.

When I was in bed, despite the darkness, I kept the blanket right over my head. This meant that my feet were sticking out the other end because I wasn't able to curl up, and thus they were rather chilly, but the point was I couldn't even begin to see into the cell next door, and they couldn't see me. Ostrich, me? Oh yes.

One of those women tried to kill me. And my baby. However much I kept saying that I thought it was Jevina (note: not however much I kept actually *thinking* it was Jevina), even though there was now apparently an eyewitness, I just wasn't totally convinced. Maybe I was just expecting things to be more difficult than that – I'm not used to solutions presenting themselves that quickly. But when you look at it logically, I suppose, criminals who are in prison are probably not the ones best known for the insolubility of their crimes.

The Wolf had said to leave it to her. I didn't like that. I'm not a natural delegator; I'm one of those big-headed control-freaky people who doesn't trust other people to do the job right. Apart from ironing. I have no problems at all with other people doing my ironing. Or the washing up. Ahem, anyway, what I'm saying is, if there was going to be an investigation into crimes against me, I had to be in charge or things were going to be missed (despite all the evidence of my recent oblivious state to the contrary). But, whatever,

I was determined to get to the bottom of it. I may have the size and general mobility on land of a giant squid, but I wasn't going to let anyone get away with what they'd done to Deedee, and tried to do to my child and I.

My dreams, during the few patches of sleep I managed to grab, were filled with revenge. When I finally woke up in the morning, my fists were clenched. I kept my gaze averted from next door still, all through the normal morning business before the doors were unlocked.

Almost the second the doors slid back, I could hear running footsteps in the corridor. Not Aseks, they never ran. The four of us went to look out, see what was going on, and we got caught up in the streaming crowd. Every cultist on the floor was heading for cell D19.

The cells aren't that big. Barely half of the crowding women could fit in. I found myself swept into next door, and scrabbled to get a hold on the smooth wall and keep out of whatever was going on. I could barely turn my head, and couldn't see where any of my cellmates were.

I spotted the Wolf in the crowd. 'What's happening?' I yelled.

'No one shall harm this baby!' she yelled back. Obviously a sentiment I shared, but...

The women were surrounding Jevina. She seemed stunned; her expression was just a bemused 'what's going on?' I'd dreamed of revenge. It was happening.

Crow and Thall, ignored by the cultists but unable to get out of the cell, scrambled on to a top bunk. So they had a bird's eye view of what was happening.

I've seen mobs lots of times. They throw punches, thump and kick and shout. But you know what? I'm going to buy into centuries of differentiation and say that that's because those mobs weren't entirely made of women. This mob was a cat fight writ large. They weren't punching, they were pulling: hair, clothes, hooking their nails into her skin. This is what I wanted to happen to the woman who'd tried to hurt my baby. This is what I wanted to *do* to the woman who'd

97

tried to hurt my baby.

But was this the woman who'd tried to hurt my baby?

This mustn't happen, not like this.

There should be proof; there should be a trial. Even if she were guilty; even if I wanted to tear her limb from limb (and I did), could I stand by and watch this happen and still call myself a member of a civilised race?

If she were guilty – maybe I could. But I *didn't know that she was*. And I really, really couldn't ever think of myself as civilised if I gave in to mob justice. Innocent till proven guilty. I believed in that, I really believed in it.

'Stop!' I was shouting. 'Stop this! I'm the Great Mother, you have to listen to me! We've no proof it's her!'

They didn't listen. They were too caught up in it. Jevina had tried, ineffectually, to fight them off. Her resistance had lasted for mere seconds before she was overwhelmed. Her screams kept being cut off as sharp fingernails raked across her face again and again. This was more than just teaching someone a lesson.

Thall had obviously worked out what was going on. 'It was her?' she was screaming. 'It was her who killed my Deedee?' She launched herself from her bunk-top perch, almost flattening a cultist, and grabbed a handful of mauvey curls.

I tried to kick my way through the crowd towards Jevina or the Wolf. Maybe I could help the one or reason with the other. Unfortunately I was unable to lift either leg much higher than ten centimetres and couldn't get much force behind them, but I managed to whack a few shins. My arms were flailing all around me like in one of those co-ordination exercises where you try to keep them both windmilling in opposite directions. Half of it was to keep me upright, the other half was a further attempt to clear a path. 'Stop! Stop!' I was yelling the whole time.

Then: 'Stop! Stop!' That was the Wolf! Victory! She was calling an end to this brutality!

Fat chance.

She was staring straight at me. 'Get her out of here!' she

shouted. 'The baby must not be harmed.'

And a bunch of them broke away from the crowd surrounding Jevina, now collapsed on the floor, panting and sobbing in this brief respite. I think that was the cruellest part of all: pausing the torture. Maybe allowing her to think, for one or two seconds, that she was going to get out of it alive.

The splinter group grabbed me. A path appeared in the mass of bodies and they dragged me out of the cell. I tried to turn my head to see what was happening as the shrieking resumed behind me, but I couldn't. As I was taken through the doorway – well, that's when I heard the sound. The one I've already described.

They bundled me into my own cell. Somehow Claire and Sophia had got swept up along the way and were suddenly with me. The cultists pulled across the door to our cell, and stood there, holding it, blocking us in. No way we could force our way out.

The slamming of the door cut off the sound. My ears were ringing, the way they do when loud noise gives way to sudden silence. But I knew that the sound was still going on.

When I knelt on my bunk, my face was only feet away from the action. Blood had splattered on the wall. I forced myself to stare through the red barrier until the end, but I didn't realise that I was still shouting until Claire put her arm around me and tried to hush me. I'd been yelling 'We don't know it's her! We don't know it's her!' and now my throat was hurting, even though it hadn't taken that long. In fact it only lasted moments after I'd left the scene, but I was watching as the blood stopped pumping and there were no more struggles. I counted that they carried on tearing Jevina apart for seventeen seconds after she died.

I kept staring forward, but my eyes refocused themselves nearer home. In the foreground I watched two drips of blood run down the wall, wondering which would reach the bottom first, like racing raindrops. Behind that was an unfocused, crumpled mass of pinky-white and red that

I didn't want to see.

Sound began again. Laughs and self-satisfied noises. I realised the door must have been opened, and tore my gaze away from the chasing blood drops. The Wolf entered our cell. 'We didn't know it was her,' I said blankly.

'It doesn't matter,' she answered.

I frowned. I didn't think that answer could possibly make sense.

She continued. 'If she was the one trying to hurt you, she can't do it anymore. If she wasn't...'

'Yes?' I said, a bit more forcefully. 'If she wasn't?'

The Wolf smiled. 'After that, do you think anyone else will dare to touch you? Whether she was guilty or not – and I think that she was – we'll achieve the desired result. Our baby is no longer at risk.'

'This is *my* baby!' I screamed at her.

Oh shit. Oh shit oh shit oh shit.

None of us had breakfast that morning. It didn't seem to bother the Aseks. Two of them came in to D19 and cleared away Jevina's body. That didn't seem to bother them either. They left Thrall and Crow to clear up the blood, though. I watched it all. It seemed important, somehow.

DAY –2, AFTERNOON.

We didn't really feel like eating at lunchtime either, but choked it down. My body was hungry, even if my mind wasn't. That seemed to be the case at almost every meal these days. But I really needed the energy. I was feeling so drained I could hardly lift the nutrition block to my mouth.

Claire and I were sitting on my bunk afterwards. My eyes were just beginning to close when she said 'Benny...' She was sounding a bit nervous.

'Yes?' I said, opening my eyes to look at her. She didn't answer, and her eyes were downcast. I gathered my wits together. 'Claire! What is it?'

100

'You don't think Jevina was the one who was trying to hurt you, do you?'

'I don't know,' I said. 'But whatever, things like… like that shouldn't be allowed to happen.'

'It's just…' She paused, then squeaked, 'It's my fault! It's all my fault!'

'Claire!' I hugged her tight. 'It's not your fault! How could you possibly think such a thing?'

'I told the Wolf you thought it was Jevina…'

'And I was the one who said that in the first place, and Gripper was the one who found out about Jevina's alleged involvement, and Sophia was the one who came running into the Wolf's cell to tell us. And none of us are to blame: none of us encouraged precipitate violent action. Not that Gripper wouldn't have if she'd thought of it, but you know what I mean. None of us are to blame, and you did less than anyone.'

And I almost meant it. Claire had said too much, yes, but I wasn't going to mention that. The Wolf would have found out anyway. And I tried to tell myself that I'd imagined the relief on Crow's face when Jevina was torn apart.

It might also be relevant that the girl Sara, the one who said she'd seen Jevina in our cell, went around looking absolutely terrified from then on. I would have questioned her, but events rather overtook us.

'Look,' I said to Claire, impotently, 'we're in a terrible place, but we're going to get out of it.' I paused. 'Admittedly, even if we do we'll then be in a galaxy taken over by evil fascists, but I suppose there must still be good points. Fascists haven't outlawed chocolate yet, have they?'

It was Claire's turn to be the positive one. 'They haven't taken over yet. As far as we know they haven't even had their big conference yet.'

'You're right!' I cried, punching the air in determination. 'They haven't won yet! And we're going to stop them! We'll sabotage the conference! Destroy the Fifth Axis! And then we'll do the show right here!'

Claire glared at me. 'Sorry,' I mumbled.

We sat in silence for a bit. After a few minutes I eased myself backwards to get some relief for my poor, aching, feels-like-I'm-an-octogenarian back. My feet were still on the floor, though; my silhouette of sharp angles and enormous bump looking like a jigsaw piece.

I heard soft footfalls: Sophia had come into the cell. Being pregnant must be a bit like being blind: your hearing gets extra good to compensate for not being able to see over the top of your gigantic stomach.

'Hello Sophia, we were just about to save the galaxy,' I called. 'Do join us.'

I heard her go over and perch on the edge of Gripper's bunk. She was obviously feeling particularly reckless.

'Query: in what way are you going to save the galaxy?' she asked. 'Supposition: you have come up with a plan to foil the Fifth Axis conference and planned attack, as well as informing the outside world of its intentions and warning them that there may be Fifth Axis agents amongst them?'

'You're almost right,' I told her. 'All except the bit where we've actually come up with the plan.'

But Claire was squeaking. 'That's it! That's it!'

'What's it?' I asked, looking round to check she hadn't just sat on something sharp.

'I have an idea, I have an idea!' she squealed.

'Well, don't keep us in suspense!' I said.

'Fifth Axis agents amongst us!'

'Um...'

'Gripper!'

'What about Gripper?'

'She's an Axis agent! She must be getting orders somehow – and getting messages out! She can pass a message out for us! She can warn the rest of the galaxy about the attack and the invasions and the bad people and everything.'

I gave her an indulgent but, it has to be said, pitying look. 'Nice idea,' I said, 'but I'm guessing Gripper won't want to destroy her bosses' entire plans just for us.'

'Oh yes,' Claire sighed. 'It's just she was being sort of nice so I didn't think.' She paused for a few seconds. 'So we kidnap her, and sit on her until she agrees to pass out a message for us!'

I couldn't help but smile at her enthusiasm. And there was something utterly endearing about someone who'd been through all Claire'd been through in the last few weeks whose top persuasion technique is to sit on someone until they give in. But it wouldn't work. 'I'm sorry, Claire,' I said. 'You're probably right about Gripper having some means of communication, but even if we could force her to get out a message, it'd never reach the people we wanted it to.' But there was something – some glimmer of hope. 'Hang on,' I said, waving my arms to shush everyone – although admittedly no one was saying anything. 'I think there's something in that.' I began to think aloud. 'We're not going to be able to get a message off planet, right?'

'Right,' echoed everybody.

'But there might – just *might* be a way to get a message to the Axis themselves. But it'd have to be a different sort of message. Maybe something that would make them reconsider their plans, or at least delay them for a bit.'

'Yes!' Claire shouted. 'That's it! We sit on Gripper until she sends out a delaying message to her bosses!'

I tried to calm her down a bit. 'Not quite,' I said. 'We need to be a bit more subtle than that. Not that sitting on people isn't a good idea in general,' I added hastily as she looked rather crestfallen. 'If we force Gripper to send a message for us, there're all sorts of problems. She might have to give code words to guarantee the veracity of what she's saying, and she leaves them off. She might just send out another message afterwards saying it's all a pack of lies. She might fight us all off and kill us. No, we have to trick her into thinking the information's real – and that she's sending it out on her own initiative.'

Sophia looked worried. 'Query: will it work?'

'I don't know,' I said honestly. 'It's all a bit of a gamble. For all we know, Gripper isn't even in contact with her bosses. Depends on how deep her cover was supposed to be. But until we come up with a better plan, let's go with it. Anything's better than doing nothing.'

'Additional query: what is the false information we wish to impart?'

I tapped the side of my nose knowingly. 'Ah,' I said. 'Now that's the clever part…'

Claire was squeaking her head off. 'Benny, you can't! It's insane! He hates you!'

'I know,' I said. 'But haven't you heard the phrase "my enemy's enemy is my friend"? He hates the Fifth Axis more than he hates me. They're the ones who put him inside.'

'But can you believe him?'

I shrugged. 'What possible reason could he have for lying? Like you say, he hates me. He's hardly going to want to cheer me up by making up stories about Axis traitors for my comfort.'

'And what does he want you to do?'

'I don't know yet. But if it's going to hurt the Fifth Axis…'

'I still don't like it,' she said. 'I really don't, Benny.'

I gave her a big hug. 'Don't you worry your furry little head about it. Everything's going to be fine.' I looked over her head. Sophia sidled into the room and gave me a thumbs up. (I'd taught her that. Apparently it means something completely different in Grellor.)

'She catch that?' I whispered.

'Confirmation: she listened to it all. She has now left.'

Claire sat down hard on my bunk. 'I was so scared!' she breathed.

I laughed. 'You were brilliant! I almost believed you myself.'

'But did Gripper believe it?' she asked.

'Now that,' I said, 'we will just have to wait and see…'

* * *

DAY –2, EVENING.

We managed several more info dumps that evening.

1) That we were worried Daglan Straklant might go to the Axis and offer to hand over his evidence of a high-ranking traitor in exchange for his freedom and possible reinstatement – and that 2) he'd only told me about the possibility of the offensive being sabotaged as a form of torture so it'd hurt when it failed; he really did hate me more than the Axis. He didn't actually want my help at all.

3) That the guy he had evidence against was so high up in the Axis organisation that Straklant wouldn't be likely to trust his information with anyone other then the Imperator himself (we thought that would definitely put the cat among the pigeons).

4) That Straklant suspected that the traitor not only intended to sabotage the entire operation, but also to assassinate the Imperator.

5) That none of us had a clue who the traitor was (covering our backs there – didn't want to be dragged off for questioning).

We added that second one because I was a bit worried that the motivations of both myself and Straklant wouldn't stand up to close examination – I mean, they're still pretty wafer thin, not to mention inconsistent, but I did come up with the plan very quickly and, basically, it's our best and possibly only shot and there wasn't time to fine tune it.

I don't know if anything will come of it. After all, chances are Gripper doesn't have any contact with her Axis bosses. But as I lay in bed I couldn't help but think of the scenario... Gripper running hastily to her Asek contact; panic spreading through the ranks of the Axis, all the way to the Imperator himself... Straklant dragged off and tortured – revealing nothing, but they cancel the attacks anyway just to make sure... The Imperator trusting no one and the whole structure crumbling... Straklant being tortured again and they don't believe he doesn't know anything so they keep torturing him...

Maybe this night I'd have pleasant dreams for once.

As a matter of fact I did, for a while. I was back on the Braxiatel Collection, lying by the lake in the sun with Jason's arms around me, and my child was playing on the grass with Wolsey. Idyllic, and to be honest quite surprising when I think of my recent relationship with Jason. And, indeed, with the sun. Strangely, I could see my child clearly in my dream, but when I woke up the picture faded away before I could grasp even the slightest detail of it. And strangest of all, at the end of my dream, just before I awoke with a shiver, it all changed tone and we were menaced by a house-sized hamster... now what was *that* saying about my psyche?

And suddenly, I realised exactly what it was saying.

You know how I said I was going to start being suspicious again? Well, it was back with a vengeance. A really unpleasant vengeance.

It was the middle of the night. I'm lying there, wishing I could get back to sleep, all the calm of my original dream destroyed utterly – the weight of the world on my shoulders. Everything seems so much worse at night. Little things come back to haunt you, things you've said or done and wish you hadn't said or done. Little things that caused big things to happen.

If I hadn't gone to see the Wolf. If I'd warned Claire beforehand not to give too much away. If only Claire hadn't mentioned Jevina...

And that was when the end of my dream became clear, and the suspicions started. The painful ones.

The Wolf: No harm is going to come to this baby.

Claire: No harm is going to come to this baby!

The Wolf: Hello Benny, Claire.

But she'd not met Claire before.

You were brought to Deirbhile.

'I'm coming with you.'

'No, Claire, you don't have to...'

'Yes I do. I was hired to look after you, and I'm going to do that whatever.'

The cult knew you were coming. 'Claire, were you using the comms link?'

We knew about the baby, about its parentage.

But no one knew the full story, no one except me, Brax, Jason, Adrian, Avril… and Claire.

My best friend's a Pakhar. Claire's just like her.

My mother was called Claire. It predisposes me towards anyone with that name.

A bit of a coincidence, a Pakhar with my mother's name.

Insisting on coming with me to see the Wolf and letting things slip. Things that caused a girl to be torn to pieces. Someone got Sara to feed us information at the crucial time.

Taking such great care of my baby. Not seeming to care about anything but my baby.

I like her so much. Love her, care for her, best girlie friends who'd be having ice cream and gossip sleepovers if we weren't in prison.

Would trust her with my life. But I've proved time and time again that I can't trust my own judgement.

What if Claire's the one who wants to take my baby away from me?

How can I find out? I can't ask her. If it's true she wouldn't tell me, and if it's not… how can you explain to someone that you thought they might be one of the bad guys? It's not the sort of thing that's easy to forgive and forget.

But I was going to have to try to forget about it. Whether she's Claire my friend or Claire the Cultist, she'll want this baby born safely. I will have to trust her with that, because, basically, I need someone who knows what they're doing.

I had to put all those terrible suspicions out of my mind, there and then. Claire was my friend.

I managed to get to sleep three hours before we had to get up.

10
Enforced Sobriety

I really need a drink.

11
Anticipation

In the morning, I dismissed it all. Of *course* Claire wasn't a spy. Of *course* Claire wasn't part of the cult. Of any cult. Of *course* she was my friend. Don't you have times like that? Something seems the biggest deal in the dead of night, and you just think 'how could I have been so stupid?' when you've had some sleep and it's daylight again.

That's one thing you can say about the Glass Prison. We're not short of daylight. No worries about east- or west-facing windows, they face north, south, east and west, and all points in between. Strangely, even after my recent... experience, seeing the sun rise still cheers me up. I was beginning to think that perhaps I wasn't a natural late-riser, as I'd previously thought – having had this tendency to stay out half the night and then sleep until the afternoon – perhaps my natural rhythms were more in tune with Mother Nature and slightly less dictated to by alcohol consumption.

For some reason, the feeling of relief wasn't the only emotion I woke up with. But I'm not sure how to describe what I felt. It's the sort of thing that I'm pretty sure you can only really empathise with if you've felt it; that defies description – but I'll try anyway. It's like... this was going to be the last day I was whole. Yes, I wanted to get to know my baby as a real little person. Yes, I wanted to be able to do all those things I used to be able to do, like run, or sleep on my stomach, or drink seventeen pints (were they available), but I would never, ever be this close to my child again. At the moment he or she was part of me. After tomorrow – assuming the Fifth Axis were right – we would be two separate people. I had to hang on to every tiny moment of this time, savour it, preserve it in my memory for ever. Every second was precious. Even the ones just lying here, listening to Sophia snoring over the other side of the room.

He or she. I did wonder which it would be. You know how people say, 'I don't care what it is, as long as it's healthy'? Well, I suppose that's true for me too. I mean, I can think of loads of reasons why I'd prefer a girl. But as I can also think of loads of reasons why I'd prefer a boy, it's not really an issue.

It's not like I'm a particularly girlie-girl, desperate to have a little daughter to dress in fairy frocks and silver shoes – which is just as well, because I'm now imagining a tiny female Adrian Wall in pink petticoats, reminding me uncomfortably of those long-outlawed chimpanzee's tea parties – but I can imagine bonding with this little version of me (albeit probably a bit furrier), teaching her the ways of women; giving her insights into the female condition; doing all these little mother-daughter things. Disapproving of her boyfriends, that sort of stuff. Or a little boy... actually, then I'd just teach him the ways of men (I think I've learned quite a lot of them over the years); give him insights into the male condition (ditto), and disapprove of his girlfriends. Or try to become their best friend, that sometimes works.

In all of this I am, of course, assuming that both my baby and I will be out of prison. Nothing else bears thinking about.

So I wouldn't think about being in prison. Wouldn't think about my baby being taken away from me. I'd think about knitting bootees, and changing nappies, and singing lullabies. About colouring books, and building blocks, and learning how to bake birthday cakes. Picnics and teddy bears and baby's first Christmas.

DAY –1, AFTERNOON

By the afternoon, I was completely knackered. Lack of sleep catching up with me. But I knew I mustn't sleep. Couldn't sacrifice these last few hours of being a Benny-baby gestalt

112

entity for the mere blessed oblivion of slumber. Unfortunately, once I'd laid down on my bunk after lunch, I just couldn't get up again, and do you know how hard it is not to fall asleep when you're totally drowsy, have just eaten (albeit not exactly well), and are lying on your bed? My eyelashes were just brushing my cheeks when my bladder began to remind me that I'd not paid any attention to it for at least three minutes. I decided to ignore it. But of course, that never works. I tried to sit up. I couldn't. I really, truly couldn't. There was just too much... tummy there.

It was true that just in the last couple of days I seemed to have expanded rather more than seemed healthy. I'd gone from pillow-up-the-jumper size to something approaching a king-size duvet, and thank the goddess that my new smock had been meant for a Terpsechian. Ladies, beware, when conceiving a child, make sure the father is not of a race of seven-foot-plus muscle-packed dog-ape creatures. Unless you are a female of the species of seven-foot-plus muscle-packed dog-ape creatures, of course. Perhaps the ballooning did mean that the end was in sight. It wasn't something Adrian had mentioned, but then we had quickly worked out that there wasn't that much correlation between the Killoran way of whelping and the human method of giving birth, so, frankly, anything could happen.

Ballooning. A completely inappropriate word. Balloons, being filled with helium, are lighter than air. Making them bigger therefore just makes them even lighter. Perhaps a better term would be 'bricking'. As I was expanding it was like someone was tying extra bricks to my belly. Of course, it also has connotations of the late twentieth-century slang term of 'bricking it'. Which, if you want it all spelled out for you, basically means I'm huge, I'm heavy, and I'm just plain scared.

'Can somebody give me a hand?' I called out. 'Or paw,' I added, as Claire peered over the edge of her bunk. Sophia came over and helped Claire down, and they took an arm each and pulled.

'Make a wish!' I gasped, feeling like the Christmas turkey (and about as agile).

'I think you know what we wish,' panted Claire. (How could I ever have suspected this lovely, lovely person?)

'Right now,' I said, 'ignoring the obvious health, wealth, happiness and falling asleep for a hundred years beloved of fairy godmothers, I wish I had a cable car that would take me from my bunk to the loo and back.'

'So do I,' Claire huffed, as I struggled upright.

They helped me to shuffle around, and eventually my feet were on the floor. 'Oooh,' I sighed. 'My feet...'

'Fact: your ankles are very swollen,' Sophia pointed out.

'I'll take your word for that,' I said. 'I haven't seen them since June.'

'Only to be expected,' said Claire in her brisk, nurse voice.

'And I suppose the needing-the-loo-every-two-minutes thing, that's only to be expected too?'

'Well, yes,' she said. 'You know it is.'

'And how about the sudden swelling to twice the size of a beachball?'

'Yes...' said Claire distractedly, as they attempted to lower me down. (I realise this may be going into more detail than you would perhaps like, but this whole loo thing is a big part of my life at the moment and if you don't want to hear about it, go follow someone else's story.)

'And if I got another wish,' I said, 'it would be that my would-be murderer ex-Kolonel Daglan Straklant couldn't see me when I'm on the bog.'

Claire's nose twitched. 'Oooh!' she said. 'That's a really odd thing. You see – he isn't there.'

'Query?' asked Sophia. 'Who is not where?'

'Straklant. He's not in his cell.'

'Are you sure?' I said.

'Mmm. You know how close I am in my bunk.' She shivered.

I wrinkled my forehead. 'But no one's allowed out during afternoon lock-in. Hey! Maybe he's been dragged off to A

114

floor! Maybe he's *dead*!' I was so pleased by the prospect that I quite forgot about my gigantic bulk. Well, for a few microseconds. 'Maybe you'd better leave me here for the afternoon,' I suggested. 'I don't think we can go through all this every five minutes.'

I am so elegant sometimes that it hurts.

DAY –1, EVENING

It was almost time for evening lock-in. Sophia was out somewhere attempting to Find Facts – in this case for us; she was trying to find out what had happened to Daglan Straklant. In a complete reversal of our normal policy, we'd kept looking upstairs since Claire's realisation, and not seen him once. I was even beginning to entertain wonderful suspicions that maybe our plan had worked; maybe he'd been dragged off for questioning and even now Fifth Axis forces across the galaxy were being recalled just in case. I had to bite my tongue and stop myself asking Gripper if that were the case; if she'd passed our fake messages on. Anyway, Sophia would be back in a moment, and if there was anything to find out, she would have found it. I had no worries about her missing lock-in. Even Sophia, lost in facts, would never dare to miss lock-in. No one did.

'Sleep tight! Looking forward to tomorrow – *mummy*?' Gripper said, cheerfully, as I got ready for bed. Which actually meant staying exactly where I was on my bunk, but pulling the blanket over me.

'We don't know it's tomorrow,' I said, unconvincingly. 'It's just guesswork. It could be months yet.'

'Let's hope not for your sake,' she said, gesturing at my waistline. 'Another few inches and you'll burst.'

'I don't think Claire would let that happen!' I said. 'Would you, Claire? Claire? Claire...?'

Claire was silent. I turned my head, to see her shuffling her paws awkwardly. I could tell she wanted to say something but didn't quite know how to start. 'What is it?' I asked her, a bit worried.

'Benny... you know how big you've got...?'

'Hmm,' I said, with a frown on my face. 'Yeah. I think I'm going to sue Galactic Weight-Watchers.'

'Benny, I'm serious,' she said, and I could see she was.

I raised myself on to one elbow as best I could. 'What is it?' I said, my stomach suddenly freezing up.

She knelt by my side and stared up at me. I could see two little reflections of myself in her enormous black eyes. 'Benny... it's all happened very suddenly. Until a day or so ago, you were a normal size for a human woman at this stage of pregnancy. But now... I hoped I was imagining it at first, but I'm not. You're bigger than a human woman at forty weeks.'

'That's... that's not a problem, is it?' I said. 'I mean, we don't know what's normal for a human-Killoran baby.'

She didn't answer for a moment. Then she said, 'Benny, lie back down. I need to examine you properly.'

I didn't ask any more questions; I lay down and pushed off the blanket. What could I say? Am I going to be all right? Is my baby going to be all right? If the answers were yes, Claire would have told me already. We wouldn't be doing this. If they weren't... I didn't want to know. Not yet.

'Looks fun,' Gripper commented from a prone position on her own bunk. 'Can anyone join in?'

'Sod off,' I told her.

Claire moved her little paws gently but firmly over my swollen belly. Normally they tickled. Right now, I didn't seem to be very ticklish. She was thorough, as always. Finally she sat back, rocking on her heels.

I could hardly bring myself to ask, 'Well?'

'I don't want you to worry...' she began.

'Too late!' I cried. 'Sorry. Sorry. I didn't mean to snap. But please, just tell me.'

'The baby is fine,' she began. 'Really it is, I'm not just saying that. And the swelling, as far as I can tell, is not a problem with you. That is to say, you are not suffering from

116

any adverse medical condition.'

'Hurrah,' I said feebly. 'Claire... you're looking pretty worried for someone who's just told me that everything's fine.'

She shook her head, and reached for my hand. 'Benny... everything isn't fine. That's not what I said. The baby is healthy and you are healthy – as far as I can tell with no facilities, that is. As you say, we don't know what's normal for human-Killoran pregnancies, but I don't think there's anything wrong with either of you. You need more nutrients, of course, but...'

'Claire! Stop beating about the bush!'

'Sorry. But what has happened, you see, is that the baby has undergone a huge and unexpected growth spurt.'

'I'd noticed,' I said. 'It must be all the chocolate buns. They're so generous at teatime and I just can't resist. Sorry. I always joke when I'm nervous. You might have noticed.'

She nodded, not, I think, taking in what I was saying. 'I suspect that the growth would normally have come on more gradually in the run up to the birth, but the baby was not getting sufficient nutrients. Now, with the birth presumably imminent, it can't wait any longer and has been snatching every scrap of energy it can to get into shape for the big day. That's probably one of the reasons you've been so tired.'

'So I'm going to have a big baby,' I said. 'It's not exactly a surprise. After all, its father is King Kong.' Of course, I knew that there had to be some problem. I was just waiting for Claire to tell me what it was.

'I think there's a serious chance of cephalopelvic disproportion.' She continued quickly before I could make a supposedly humorous comment. 'That means I think the baby's head is too big to pass safely though your pelvis.'

'Oh,' I said. 'So... oh goddess, you mean I really will burst?'

'No – snip snip snip!' called Gripper. I glanced over. She was making scissor actions with her fingers.

'Since when were you a childbirth expert?' I snapped at

her. But Claire was nodding.

'Yes, it would normally involve a caesarean section.'

'Normally?' I asked.

'Well… always,' Claire said. 'It's just that…'

'We're in prison?'

'Yes,' she said. 'That's the problem.'

'And what happens…?'

'Don't ask what happens if the operation can't take place,' said Claire. 'It has to. We'll have to tell the Aseks. The authorities are going to have to let you out.'

'Because, of course, the Fifth Axis will be overjoyed at having all their plans overturned,' Gripper put in.

'They'll *have* to do something,' Claire said.

'Really? I reckon mother and baby dying in childbirth'd do just as well for them,' said Gripper. 'Fate against the prophecy, all tha–'

Claire was on top of her before I'd barely registered the movement. 'Shut up!' she was yelling. 'Shut up! Benny's going to be fine! The baby's going to be fine! Nothing is going to harm this baby!' She jumped up as quickly as she'd leapt in the first place. 'I'm going to find an Asek. They have to help us.'

I was struggling to sit up as she sped out of the door.

'I wouldn't bother trying to catch up with her,' Gripper said from her still-relaxed position. 'They'll throw her back in in a minute. Well, either that or chuck her downstairs to A floor. And what happens if you drag yourself outside and don't have the energy to drag yourself back in again? You'll miss lock up.'

'Shut up,' I muttered, trying to get my legs over the side of the bunk. I shuffled my bottom across, and after a few seconds my left leg was half-suspended somewhere between the bunk and the floor. A moment later I managed to get my right leg around to join it. I tried to sit up. On the first attempt, my upper back made it about an inch and a half above the horizontal, then I collapsed back down. Second attempt, about the same. 'You might offer to give me a hand,' I called across to Gripper, now leaning on one elbow watching me with every indication of enjoyment.

'Nah,' she said.

On the third attempt I managed a lift of three inches. Unfortunately, with my legs still in mid air, this altered my centre of gravity and I began to slide inexorably towards the floor. Could I catch myself? No, I could not. Agility is just something that happens to other people these days. Luckily the friction between the blanket and my smock made the progress slow enough that I landed with only a very small bump. Gripper was still observing me like I'd been provided for her very own in-cell entertainment. And from my semi-supine position I noticed the guy upstairs had stopped mid press up to check what was going on. He gave me a little wave of encouragement. I waggled my fingers back.

Sophia arrived back before Claire. 'I have found facts! I have found facts!' she called.

'Brilliant!' I said. 'What facts would these be, then?'

You could tell Sophia was in an ecstatic state where nothing but her precious facts mattered. She didn't even ask me what I was doing on the floor.

'Fact: Daglan Straklant was taken from E floor by the Aseks shortly before lunch. He is now in a holding cell on A floor!'

'That's fantastic!' I cried. 'Something must be happening! Something... good!' I couldn't say any more because of Gripper. Damn, damn, damn. I really wanted to talk this over. Lucky that Claire came back and distracted me.

This was a new Claire. She had her paws on her hips and was looking very determined and efficient. 'All sorted,' she said.

I could hardly believe it. 'I'm going to a hospital?!' I cried.

Her arms and face dropped. 'No. Sorry. They wouldn't agree to that. But they're going to bring in a doctor and medical equipment. Tomorrow morning.'

My face dropped too, but I tried to hide my disappointment. 'Oh well, at least that's something.'

'It is, Benny, it is,' Claire insisted. 'Oh, I dread to think what would happen if you went into labour without appropriate medical resources...'

'Er, yeah.'

She gave herself a shake. 'Sorry. Sorry.' Then she smiled. 'No need to dwell on that. It's going to be okay. Um, Benny...?'

'Yes,' I said, with a sense of further dread.

'Why are you sitting on the floor?'

12
You Can't Always Get What You Want

Everyone is asleep. I have wanted to sleep all day, and now I've decided it's okay, I can't. There's – unsurprisingly – a lot to think about.

Being a mother. It's something I'm going to have to make up as I go along. You don't get a practice session beforehand. And it's not as if I even had much of a chance to watch it in action during my own childhood. Not that I'm going to start moaning and feeling sorry for myself – well, not more than usual, anyway. I do feel I missed out on something special, but, if I'm in a silver-lining mood, I suppose I'm lucky in some ways too. At least I had a mother, if only for a few years. And at least she was wonderful, and sweet, and caring. Do you know how I lost her? It was during the war, and we were running into the shelter. I dropped my favourite doll. I really loved that doll. It's one of those peculiarly human things: the ability to invest an inanimate object with qualities deserving of affection. A thing of rag and buttons and cotton stuffing is more of a person to you than the woman who lives down the road. Nowadays, with AI's everywhere, it's even worse. Joseph, for example, my little electronic porter. He's a person. Oh, I know he's just a collection of wires and circuits, but even so... Of course, I'm speaking as someone who has frequent altercations with her coffee maker, so perhaps I'm not the best person to have this philosophical discussion with. Sheesh, do I digress or what?

My favourite doll. My constant companion. Sharer of tea-parties (I wasn't allowed caffeinated beverages, so we drank orange juice with a drop of milk and two lumps of sugar. Pretty disgusting, but it made me feel grown up); wearer of

121

pillow-case dresses and bearer of nail-scissor haircuts and felt-tip make-up. How could I bear childhood without her? But in the hurry and scurry and panic and terror I dropped her on the ground. And my selfless, beautiful, wonderful mother went back to get her. I didn't want her to! I may have loved my doll, but I loved my mother more! Why why why did she have to go, to leave me like that? Mummy, I'd have given up a thousand dolls for you, a million. I'd have given up anything to have you back.

So what I know is, being a good mother means caring for your child. Loving it. Walking that thin line between allowing sweets and maintaining healthy teeth and gums. Kissing grazed knees and banishing tears. Rescuing toys, but not dying. Being a good mother means being there with your child, throughout. I have to do that. No one's going to separate us, no way. Whatever it takes.

DAY 0, MORNING

I woke up on Saturday utterly unable to believe that I might be about to give birth. In the end I'd lain awake half the night, unable to reconcile my feelings about the thing inside me. Part of me was still thinking of it as an alien intruder, and was desperate to get it out of me, not to mention wanting to be able to walk normally again and have an 'inny' belly button instead of this weird sticky-outy one. The rest... well, the rest of me was so desperately attached to it, considering it a part of me, unwilling to be separated from it even as part of the natural process to allow it to become itself. Once it was out there... oh goddess, I would have created life. It wouldn't be part of me any more, it would be a separate little creature with its own desires and thoughts and dreams. Not mine. And I would no longer be Bernice Summerfield, I would be Bernice Summerfield: mother. Everything – *everything* – I did would have to take someone else into account. This someone. This bit of my life.

I wonder, if I'd been in a lovely (non-prison) hospital,

would they have given me some nice tranqs to make the nasty feelings go away? Still, at least I'd be getting a doctor today, even if he was going to slice me open.

Sophia saw me trying to sit up, and jumped out of her bunk to help.

At least after today I'd be the one looking after someone again, not the one who needed looking after. Unassisted movement, here I come.

I waddled over to the washstand, and poured a drop of liquid from the jug on to a torn scrap of smock. It didn't fizz, so I splashed the water over my face. Unsurprisingly, we were all a touch paranoid still, even after the lynching and the Wolf's assurances.

Behind me, Sophia was helping Claire down. On the other side of the cell, Gripper was stretching and yawning. She grinned when she saw me. I wasn't comforted: a lot of deadly things smile at you just before they pounce. She did the 'scissors' mime again.

'A caesarean is nothing to worry about,' said Claire for the umpteenth time, shooting a glare at Gripper. 'They'll give you a local anaesthetic, make the incision, and take out the baby. It'll only take minutes.'

'Major surgery, I thought it was,' Gripper commented.

I ignored her. I was only glad that these days you're allowed to eat before operations. I always need to eat when I'm panicking. Of course, high-cal, low-nutrition comfort food is usually on the menu rather than grey nutrition gunk, but right now anything would do. I just needed the energy.

The four of us readied ourselves for the day ahead – not that that involved much. As far as I could see on all sides, women were lining up, hanging around the locked doors waiting to be let out for a few hours of the closest thing we'd get today to freedom.

Several Aseks walked past, and then a few minutes later another passed in the opposite direction. Nearly time for unlocking. I wondered, not for the first time, if the Aseks felt anything at all – the shifts changed over while we were (theoretically) asleep: minimum fuss and no worries about the entrance being opened while there were prisoners on the loose. Did the retiring Aseks feel content at the thought of a day's work well done? Did the incoming shift feel excited about the new challenges the day might bring? Did Aseks have off-days, when they'd rather stay in bed and watch daytime TV? Who could tell.

The doors slid back, right on time. Claire and Sophia helped me along – they'd offered to try to sneak out some rations for me but I didn't want them to risk it, and anyway I was sick of lying in bed. I noticed in passing that a few of the women were carrying plastic beakers with them, and thought it a bit odd – there's usually plenty provided. But the Aseks didn't stop them, so it wasn't perceived as a problem. There also seemed to be a bit of tension in the air – fool that I am, I put it down to projection: I was feeling so freaked out by the possibility of giving birth that I was sensing stress everywhere. Hormones again, I told myself stupidly. Or maybe this time it was pheromones. Something like that, anyway.

We reached the dining room. Women were queued up at the food machine, a few already sat at benches, some hanging around in groups, chatting. The customary ten Aseks were stationed around the walls, watching everything. Claire, Sophia, Gripper and I headed over to the food queue. I noticed the Wolf was in the queue, standing with a group of beaker-holding cultists, all holding beakers, and thought it odd that she was getting her own breakfast. Normally someone fetched it for her. I wondered idly and ridiculously if it was to do with the baby – if she were choosing to show humility on the day of its birth, something like that.

You know how I mentioned earlier how my hormones were making me really slow?

As soon as I was comfortably inside the room – at least, that seemed to be the trigger – the tension suddenly increased so much that the air was humming: my hair was standing on end. And the Wolf shouted, 'Now!'

In an instant, everything changed. Cultists filled the doorways, blocking all exits. I found myself surrounded on all sides – not threatening-surrounded, but protective-surrounded. Each group of beaker-clutching cultists took on an Asek, throwing the contents on to its face. Acid. There were inhuman screams. Guess that sort of answers one of my questions about the Aseks – they could, at least, feel pain. The shrieking Aseks were knocked to the floor, hands tied behind their backs with plaited ropes made from smock material. Other Aseks had come up to the doors, but the cultists were keeping them at bay. Guess this might be the first time the Aseks regretted not carrying weapons – if, of course, they were capable of feeling regret. Some of the non-cultist women, obviously surprised to start with, took advantage of the situation and began to lay into the wounded Aseks. Other women huddled by the benches, trying to keep out of the way. I noticed that, even in an extreme situation like this, the prisoner's instinct was to keep away from the sides of the room. The normal reaction would be to back into a corner, but in the Glass Prison you never did that. You felt like there was a thousand foot drop behind you. It was illogical – the walls weren't going to collapse, and the only difference between this and a normal building was that you could see the drop – but it was instinctive and everyone did it.

The Wolf walked over to a whimpering Asek. Its face was not pleasant to look at, but I don't think the acid had done the damage it would have to a human. Their skins must be tougher, like Grel hide. Its eyes were milky white, no different from before, but I got the impression that it wouldn't see again. I felt a stab of pain for the Asek. It was inhuman and uncaring, but I don't think it deserved this.

Two cultists pulled the creature to its knees. It was almost face to face with the Wolf, not that it would know that. She produced something from inside her smock. I almost laughed – but swallowed it back. What she had was a sharpened toothbrush, still with bristles at one end. A prison weapon.

She held the point to the Asek's throat. It wouldn't know it was a toothbrush, that it'd probably snap in half if she tried anything, the Asek would just feel the sharpness.

'Tell me the door codes,' she said. 'I want the codes to open and lock internal doors, and the ones to open all communicating passages between floors.'

The Asek didn't say anything.

'You don't get a second chance,' she said. 'Tell me now, or I will kill you. I have nine of your colleagues here, and eventually one of them will tell me. But you will still be dead.'

The Asek still didn't say a word. Was it calling her bluff? Please let it tell her, I was thinking. Get this over with. We'll get out of here and no harm done. I looked at its streaming eyes. Well, no more harm done. And how could she play this? Her toothbrush bluff hadn't worked…

I was still looking at the Asek's expressionless white eyes when she drove the point into one. It went so deep that eyeball fluid was coating the bristles when she pulled it out. The Asek collapsed backwards with a faint cry. 'Next one,' she said.

Oh goddess, she hadn't been bluffing after all.

'What the hell are you doing?' I shouted, before my brain had time to point out what a bad idea it was to cross a toothbrush-wielding maniac. And perhaps I was being hypocritical, because I'd once killed someone like that. Only I'd used a paintbrush. And it hadn't been in cold blood either. And I hadn't enjoyed it, and had never done it again since. So, actually, no, I wasn't being hypocritical, and it was perfectly acceptable for me to shout at the Wolf. 'Stop doing that!' I yelled.

She glanced over at me. 'We're making sure the birth goes smoothly,' she said. 'You should be grateful.'

'Have you ever heard that what a baby experiences in the womb can affect it for life?' I said. 'What sort of start do you think this child is going to have if it's forced to witness a massacre just before it enters the world?'

She actually appeared to think about that one. 'It will emerge ready to fight. It will grow up knowing that violence is sometimes the only way. It will know when to make a stand. It will be prepared for life.'

'But I don't want it to live like that!' I yelled, incensed.

'It doesn't matter what you want,' she replied. 'This baby belongs to us. Bring me the next one.' And she'd turned away, dismissing me like I was some minor but necessary irritation: the cashier at the baby shop, the carrier bag to take the child home in.

I felt Claire move beside me, and grabbed hold of her smock. Didn't want her going anywhere near the Wolf in this mood. Her little legs kept running even though I was making her stay still. 'If you keep on like this there won't *be* any baby!' she shouted at the cultists. 'Without a doctor, Benny and the baby will both die!'

Shit. I knew that from what she'd already said, it's just… that was rather a stark way of putting it.

The Wolf actually paused, and turned back to us. 'Is this true?' she asked me.

'Yes,' I said, forcing myself to speak calmly. 'It's not as straightforward as we had expected. The baby will not be able to come out normally. I need a caesarean section, and for that I need a doctor. The Aseks had arranged for one to arrive today. This morning. He could be in the building now.'

'Right.' That seemed to decide her. 'We'd better get on with this. Sooner we get to A floor, sooner we can get your doctor up here.' She moved on to another Asek. I tried to push my way through the barrier of cultists, but they weren't letting me go and I didn't have the strength to force it. Claire and Sophia were being held back too, now, and neither of them were exactly built for fighting. Gripper, who was built for fighting, wasn't even trying. 'Surely you should be doing something?' I yelled at her.

She shrugged. 'I'm not getting in the way of this lot. They seem to know what they're doing.'

There was a screech. The second Asek had fallen to the Wolf's homemade spike.

'Just tell her the codes!' I pleaded to the remaining guards. But five more died before she got them.

There were whoops of delight from the cultists. They began to swarm out of the doors and call out. I could see through the walls more cultists approaching, herding Aseks before them. The Aseks were pushed through one of the dining room doors, and the remaining women went out the other, Gripper among them. The other three of us were escorted out by a group including the Wolf. I saw her send off one of the women, and a few moments later the dining room doors slammed shut. The cultists cheered again. Through the dining room walls I could see the healthy Aseks crowding round their injured brothers. Compassion? Perhaps if they'd shown some to the prisoners, this wouldn't be happening. No, it probably still would. Things are never that black and white.

Claire, Sophia and I were taken to our own cell. 'We thought it would be the most comfortable place for you, Great Mother,' said Marianne, who was one of the escort party.

'I need a doctor,' I said dully.

'The Wolf will sort it all out.'

'Oh yeah? What if the doctor's not arrived yet? What if someone's raised the alarm and they've evacuated A floor? You've got to let me out of here.'

She shook her head. She still had a beamy smile on her face. 'Benny, this is the prophesied child! Anything that happens is supposed to happen. It will all turn out all right.' Fatalism. Fine in me, extremely irritating in other people.

Claire knelt down beside me as I lay down on my bunk. I clasped my hands around my belly. 'Claire... my baby's going to die.'

She shook her head fiercely. 'No, Benny, no! This siege can't last for long. We don't know for sure you'll go into labour today – it's just some rumour by people who've never even met you! We'll wait this out, and when it's all over you'll get your doctor. Everything will be all right. Just hold on.'

And then my waters broke.

13
If I Die Before I Wake

Your waters breaking is a very strange sensation. You don't feel it at all, there are no muscles or nerves involved, and so no clue it's about to happen. One moment everything's normal, the next there's a sudden flood of warm fluid between your legs. The sort of thing that an adolescent would find hilarious.

'So, Claire,' I said, as the cult women ran about snatching up blankets and fetching jugs of water, 'this probably means it's starting, huh?'

She nodded. After a short silence, she said, 'First labour in human women usually lasts for a very long time. It will be hours before there is any danger.'

'I wish the doctor were here,' I said. Those who know me well will know just how much I meant that.

'We don't even know what's going on in the rest of the building,' Claire said.

The rest of the building. Oh goddess. 'Straklant!' I yelled. 'What if they let Straklant out! He'll kill us!'

Marianne came running over at my shout. 'No, no, Great Mother!' she insisted, trying to embrace me (I pushed her off), 'we will let no evil near you. This the Wolf has sworn!'

'Yeah, yeah, and I trust her so much aaaaah!'

'Benny?'

I tried to ease myself up so I could grasp my back. Didn't work, though.

'Benny, are you having a contraction?'

I hissed through my teeth, 'That would be when you suddenly feel that you have a tremendous stomach ache and back ache all at once, would it?'

'Well, it can be like that…'

'Then yes I am.' I sighed deeply as the cramp subsided. 'So, I've got more of those to look forward to before I die,

131

have I?'

I saw sudden tears spring up in Claire's eyes and felt horribly guilty. 'Claire! Claire, I'm a horrid old thing! I know you won't let anything happen to me. It's just... I daren't take things seriously. It's too scary.'

And that was half true and half false. If I couldn't be flippant, I'd start to think about what could really happen to me, to my baby, and I'd collapse. But the bit I was less sure about was that Claire could save me from all the horror. I knew she'd try. But she was one small cuddly bundle of niceness – I had completely dismissed all my ridiculous suspicions as night phantoms – against the combined forces of a cult, a hideous military organisation, and all the forces of nature. The odds were not, as far as I could see, in her favour.

'If only we knew what was going on,' Claire murmured. 'The gentlemen still seem to be on their own floors –' she indicated upwards – 'but goodness knows what's happening downstairs.'

'Oi,' I called, rudely, to Marianne (I was rather past caring about my public relations image at this point). 'What's going on out there? Has anyone let the men out? Are there riot police outside? What?'

She smiled at me. I gritted my teeth and imagining punching out hers. 'There is nothing to worry about, Great Mother. The Way of the Mother shall be triumphant,' she told me.

Now I was imagining wringing her smug neck. 'I don't give two hoots about your stupid, ridiculous, self-delusional cult!' I yelled. And then I tried speaking slowly and patiently, spelling it all out for her. 'The things I care about are these. That I have a baby, safely, and with a doctor in attendance. That no one tries to kill me. That is all. Nothing else, at this moment, matters to me in the slightest. But in order for these two, quite straightforward things to happen, I need to know the following: whether a doctor is here, and whether the man who wants to kill me, Daglan Straklant, has been let out of the holding cell on floor A.'

Marianne gave an apologetic shrug. 'Alas, I do not know, Gre–'

'THEN GET OUT OF HERE!' I screamed. 'Preferably go and find out what I want to know and ensure that the doctor is brought here and Straklant is kept away – and no muddling up the two with hilarious consequences, thank you very much – but at the very least will you and all your sheeplike friends get the hell out of here and just leave me in peace!'

She didn't even look taken aback. And I'll swear she wasn't going to budge, until Claire said to her: 'This amount of stress before birth could cause enormous damage to the child. *Your* child. You had better leave.'

'IT IS NOT THEIR CH–' I began, but Claire shot me such a frustrated 'I'm-lying-to-get-their-co-operation' look that I squirmed back on the pillow.

Thankfully, this apparent threat to my baby did the trick. Marianne and her cronies all shuffled out of the cell. A couple still lurked in the corridors, though.

'Thank you,' I said to Claire, taking deep, calming breaths. 'I needed that.'

She gave me a sad half-smile. 'We still don't know what's going on out there, though.'

Sophia had been standing by in slightly nervous silence during all this. She'd been looking awkward, obviously not sure what to do, but suddenly she straightened up. 'It is the duty of all Grel to find facts!' she declared. 'Fact: I have no dataxe. Yet further fact - and it is a good fact: I can still find facts to aid my non-Grel friends!' And she turned and ran out of the door.

'Sophia! Be careful!' I yelled after her. 'Oh goddess,' I said to Claire. 'We've just let off a loaded Grel. Do you think she'll be okay?'

'Of course she will,' Claire said in that way you reassure invalids when you've not got a clue really. But I appreciated the sentiment.

About two minutes later all the alarms went off.

133

* * *

From my position (flat out on bunk, stomach as high as an elephant's eye), I couldn't see anything that was going on outside our cell. If I turned my head one way I could see into D19 and the cells beyond it, and if I turned it the other way I could see into D21 and on until the corridor, but as all cells were empty in both directions that didn't help much. 'I wonder exactly what the alarms mean,' I said to Claire.

'Oh, I can tell you that,' said Gripper, wandering in. 'It means the prison systems have realised there's been a breach of security. Someone probably tried to input the wrong code; something like that. You don't get a second chance in here – after all, Aseks never make mistakes. All entrances and exits will have been sealed. Internal doors will still respond to standard codes, but external doors will require a master-override, and only a very few Fifth Axis members will know that. *I* don't know it.'

'What about a doctor?' I said. 'Would a doctor know it?'

She chuckled. 'I wouldn't have thought so for a moment.'

I gaped. 'So... we could be stuck in here for ever?'

'No!' cried Claire. Then she turned to Gripper. 'Surely not?' she asked, sounding scared.

Gripper shrugged. 'I doubt it. Although the comms-exclusion zone does mean that no one outside will know about the alarm...'

'Oh goddess.'

'But I expect the news will get out. It's not as if no one ever comes here, and it's certainly not as if you can't see what's going on inside. Someone may have been leaving the prison when the alarms went off. Or maybe your doctor will get half way here and hear the noise. Whatever, it won't be long before we're surrounded by troops. Storm the place. Take no prisoners.'

And of course, she didn't sound upset about that in the slightest.

Suddenly there was a cheer from outside. A *male* cheer. 'The troops!' Claire squeaked, panicked.

Gripper put her head against the far wall and stared hard, a hand shielding her eyes from the filtered sunlight. 'Nope,' she said eventually. 'Male prisoners. They've just discovered the door's been opened.'

She looked upwards, so did Claire. I stuck my head out over the side of the bed and looked up too. We could see a lot of shoe-soles travelling very fast. The news must be spreading quickly. My press-up friend was directly above us – he glanced down and obviously spotted us. He gave me a thumbs-up, then raced off with all the others.

'What if they come down here!' I gasped. 'Straklant could be in league with any of them! Plus they're probably all evil murderers!'

'They're not likely to come in here,' drawled Gripper, sounding bored.

'But what if they do?! What if they do?!'

Gripper wandered over to the door and sighed. 'I'll make sure they don't.'

Goodness. That I hadn't expected.

'I'm not doing it for you,' she clarified. 'Obviously. I just don't want any more complications. I should have been out of here tonight. You give birth, my job's done. I'm hoping that might still be the case.'

She left.

'Well, there's a turn up,' I said. 'The Fifth Axis: my gallant protector-aaaaaaaaaaagh!'

As I writhed on the bed, a cultist stuck her head nervously round the door to see what was going on. 'It's a perfectly natural and beautiful event!' I screamed at her. She withdrew hurriedly. They were still watching me through the wall, admittedly, but it's the thought that counts.

'I don't think I can take many more of those...' I gasped to Claire.

'Let's check you,' she said.

So few words for such an undignified procedure. It's a good job I've never been one for standing on ceremony. Of course, just at the moment, I couldn't stand on anything.

My cervix was barely dilated, Claire reported – a good thing. I was praying that a doctor got here before labour was particularly advanced. I was praying that a doctor got here at all...

My contractions were now lasting about forty-five seconds each. Doesn't sound much, does it? Less than a minute, after all. Yeah. Let's count it, shall we? Come on, with me:

One second.
Two seconds.
Three seconds.
Four seconds.
Five seconds.
Six seconds.
Seven seconds.
Eight seconds.
Nine seconds.
Ten seconds.
Eleven seconds.
Twelve seconds.
Thirteen seconds.
Fourteen seconds.
Fifteen seconds.
Sixteen seconds.
Seventeen seconds.
Eighteen seconds.
Nineteen seconds.
Twenty seconds.
Twenty-one seconds.
Twenty-two seconds.
Twenty-three seconds.
Twenty-four seconds.
Twenty-five seconds.
Twenty-six seconds.
Twenty-seven seconds.
Twenty-eight seconds.
Twenty-nine seconds.

Thirty seconds.
Thirty-one seconds.
Thirty-two seconds.
Thirty-three seconds.
Thirty-four seconds.
Thirty-five seconds.
Thirty-six seconds.
Thirty-seven seconds.
Thirty-eight seconds.
Thirty-nine seconds.
Forty seconds.
Forty-one seconds.
Forty-two seconds.
Forty-three seconds.
Forty-four seconds.
Forty-five seconds.
There. That's how long each stab of pain lasts. And Claire says they'll get longer as labour progresses. Hurrah.

14
More Pain

My contractions did get longer. They also got closer together. So I was extremely relieved – as was Claire – when Sophia returned, accompanied by a short, stocky human man. Behind them, a number of threatening-looking cultists filled the doorway, makeshift weapons in their hands. The man was about fifty years old, with black, slicked-back hair, and was wearing the dark red and silver uniform of the Fifth Axis. 'Information: this is the doctor for Bernice and her baby!' she called out.

Claire ran over and shook his hand. 'Thank goodness you're here, doctor. The contractions are fifteen minutes apart. You've probably been told that the baby is part-Killoran, and there has been rapid foetal growth in the last thirty-six hours leading to cephalopelvic disproportion and the need for a c-section.'

The doctor nodded. I waited to see what he would say next. Then I noticed. 'Hang on a second,' I said, 'where's your bag?'

'My bag?' he said. His voice was quiet and deep and calm.

Mine wasn't. 'Your doctor's bag – or whatever you brought all your stuff in. You know, the stuff you need to stop me and my baby from dying?'

'I'm sorry,' he said, spreading his hands. 'I have nothing.'

'You WHAT?!'

He seemed unconcerned. 'It was being brought in by my assistant. He was... a little way behind me. He had not yet entered the prison at the time the exits were sealed.'

'So he might have gone to get help? Yes, of course. They'll take back the prison and hand over any anaesthetics and sutures they happen to have around the place.'

Sophia was looking uncomfortable. 'You are not being realistic, Bernice. If the Fifth Axis troops do arrive, they will unfortunately probably not be concerned with helping you. Prisoners are holding the ground floor. They have killed most of the Aseks, additionally the Fifth Axis security guards who were accompanying this physician. They would have killed him also: luckily my presence and enquiry as to whether he was the expected physician led to his safe deliverance.'

'Well phew for you, Sophia,' I said, and I really, really meant it. 'Thank you. But... how can you perform a caesarean with no facilities?' I asked the doctor. Note how I'm suddenly being all polite and friendly to a member of the Fifth Axis? Shows how life-threatening situations can affect you.

He still seemed unconcerned. He turned to Claire, obviously divining her expertise. 'Do you have much experience of caesareans...?'

'Claire. I have assisted at approximately twenty c-sections, but only a quarter of those have involved human mothers.'

He looked back at me, thoughtfully, but was still addressing Claire. 'You have been monitoring the situation, Claire. How would you assess it?'

She was very calm and collected. 'I would say we have several hours before the situation becomes critical. Nevertheless, in my opinion the early the operation can be carried out, the better.

'I agree,' the doctor said. 'Nevertheless, I think we should wait. There is, of course, the possibility that this situation will end and we will have access to proper equipment. No need to court danger until it is unavoidable.'

It was now unavoidable.

Those were incredibly slow hours. S...l...oooooooowwww. Boredom relieved only by rapidly increasing contractions (which were themselves fairly boring, actually, in as much as pain can be). The doc hadn't even got so much as a paracetamol on him, which is pretty bad in my opinion. Frankly, any doctor who doesn't carry in his pockets at all times a good supply of pain killers, a shot or two of anaesthetic, a couple of sterilised scalpels and a pack of dissolving stitches ought to be disbarred. In fact, I would be informing the Fifth Axis medical council of this, just as soon as I was released from prison. And possibly shortly after I saved the world again. Because, you know, I'm certainly intending to.

I was not particularly comfortable. Sophia had rigged up blanket-strip stirrups hanging from Claire's bunk, and my feet were suspended in the air. Anyone who passed by our cell got a glorious technicolour view of my normally hidden nether regions. The stirrups reminded me of something, and I mentioned the fact to Sophia. It turns out she'd used the noose that had been left in our cell as a threat. 'For as it is said, by humans, "waste not, want not",' she told me. I *really* wish I'd never given her that talk on human sayings…

The doc seemed okay for a Fifth Axis guy. Not the sort of man I'd suddenly decide to run off with, or even become vague friends with, but he seemed pretty composed and practical, if rather pessimistic, which is about the best I could hope for under the circumstances. I don't think Claire was hugely impressed, but she was just relieved that she didn't have to bear the burden alone.

'How long since the last one?' she asked me, as a particularly noteworthy contraction hit my stomach.

'I haven't been timing it!' I yelped, rather more accusingly than I had intended.

'I know,' she said, soothingly. 'I think it's been about seven minutes. Do you agree?'

'I haven't a clue,' I answered, lapsing into sulk mode. 'I was too busy concentrating on not dying. Doesn't Dr Doom have a watch?'

'Alas, Dr Doom does not,' said the gentleman in question. 'A shame, as it would be useful.'

'Well, yes. There are lots of things which would be useful right now,' I pointed out. 'Unfortunately, the nice Axis people decided to confiscate everything we owned at the point when they decided for no very good reason that we

141

were spies and they were going to lock us up.' I sighed. 'What I wouldn't give to have Joseph back right now.'

'Joseph? This is the father of your child?' said the doctor.

I would have laughed if I'd had the energy. 'No,' I said. 'Whatever you may have heard, even I don't go for small mechanical devices.' There was a pause, as Claire gave me a raised-eyebrow look. 'Not for lasting relationships, anyway,' I added. 'Joseph is my porter, an annoying but exceedingly useful storer of data, communicator, and teller of time in both local and distant time zones, amongst many other things.'

The doctor looked exceedingly interested. 'So this device would be capable of timing your contractions, possibly monitoring your vital signs... and communicating with outside?'

'Yes, yes and no,' I told him. 'The prison's in a communications exclusion zone, didn't you know that?'

'Yes, yes. But no problem is insurmountable,' he said. I looked up at him with new respect. Not that I cared, as he probably did, that an Axis prison was in the hands of the enemy – its enemy, not so much mine – all I was thinking of was the possibility of a lovely anaesthetic and a safe delivery.

'You'll never get near the tech stuff on A floor,' I said, all the while trying to think of ways around what I was saying. 'It would have been automatically locked up when the alarms went off, and the cultists aren't going to let you wander around doing what you will, anyway.' But it would be so wonderful – if we could only get contact with the world outside Deirbhile, the bit of the world containing Irving Braxiatel, who would deal with the proposed Axis attacks and swoop down and rescue me 'n' Claire 'n' baby into the bargain. We'd given up hope now – not that we'd been talking about it in front of this Axis doctor guy, but from the veiled comments we'd allowed ourselves to make – that our cunning plan of leaking info via Gripper was going to work out. Even if she did have a way of communicating with her bosses, and even if she had passed on our false rumours about Straklant as we'd hoped (especially following his incarceration on A floor), what could possibly happen now? No one was getting in or out, so it was irrelevant. Would they trust the information enough to put their plans on hold, thinking there was a traitor? Maybe. It was our only hope.

I wondered if when Axis found out what was going on here, it might cause them to halt their conference. No. Probably not. What's a piffling little prison riot when you've got a galaxy to conquer? But there were probably security teams outside already. Preparing to move in. Any second now they would storm the place. And then they'd get me to a hospital. And not kill us at all.

'If one had this device, one could access the prison systems remotely...' the doctor was saying.

'But what good will that do?' asked Claire. 'Do you know the codes to open the main doors? Let us out?'

'No,' he said. And smiled. 'Of course, you are not forgetting you are prisoners?'

She gave him an evil look. I would have too, if I'd had the energy.

'No, I do not have the codes – I am, after all, only a doctor – but every little helps. If we can gain access to the computers, there may be a way of overriding the communication systems... and, of course, as a doctor, my responsibility would then be to you, my patient. You needn't fear any... reprisals. So tell the cult you need this communications device,' he said. 'But say it is for medical reasons – which is true enough. Do not mention it is a communications device.'

'Yes,' I said. 'I need Joseph. Sophia?'

She turned to go. 'Wait,' said Dr Doom. 'Perhaps I should go with you. You may need my assistance.'

'Query: why?'

'Because this is a Fifth Axis building and I am a member of the Fifth Axis. I think I am more likely to be able to... find my way around than a bunch of criminals.'

143

You could almost see the atmosphere freeze up.

He smiled slightly. 'No offence.'

Fifth Axis. Never trust them, even if they seem reasonable.

Another contraction hit. 'Sophia, just go!' I gasped. 'Please!'

She hurried out.

A short-ish time later she hurried back in. 'Unfortunate fact: the cultists are unable to gain entry to the store of prisoners' possessions. There is a code which they cannot break. Therefore I cannot get Joseph for you.'

'Bugger,' I muttered. 'Joseph could probably break it, but we'd have to break the code to get him out so he could break the code to get him out. Bum, bum, bum.' And then, knowing what I was really asking and hating myself for it, I said: 'Have they tried asking the Aseks?'

Sophia nodded. 'They claim not to know, despite the Wolf's attempts to find out. They say they have told her all the codes they knew. These are emergency-activated codes, they say they are not issued to the Aseks. Eventually, the Wolf appeared to believe them.'

'This is ridiculous!' stormed the doctor. 'Don't they understand what's at stake here? Let me go down. I am sure I could break this code.' He strode purposefully towards the open door.

A couple of cultists immediately leapt from their casual positions outside, blocking his way. 'You are not to leave the Great Mother,' one of them said.

'I am trying to help her!' he raged. 'You must let me down to A Floor.'

But they stood firm.

'Oh, go on!' I called out, but it changed into 'oh goaaaaaah' as another contraction shuddered through me.

Claire scampered over to the doctor and pulled at his sleeve. 'Please don't leave Benny,' I heard her say. 'She needs you, doctor.'

From what I could tell, the doctor didn't seem happy

about this at all. I wasn't fooled that he was particularly concerned for me; he just saw Joseph as a potential way of getting out of here. But as I wanted to get out of here too, that didn't worry me as much as it would under other circumstances. As long as he didn't sod off and leave me to have this baby by myself.

Or, as I didn't want to admit but knew was the reality of the situation, leave me to die.

I shuddered as the contraction subsided. The doctor and the cultists were still arguing. Claire had come over to hold my hand, and I hadn't even noticed. Suddenly the sounds from the corridor faded. 'The doctor!' I yelled. 'Where are they taking my doctor?'

Claire shushed me. 'It's all right.'

'Fact: the Fifth Axis doctor has convinced the cultists that the Aseks do know the code to the storeroom, and that he will be able to persuade them to reveal it, without resorting to what he refers to as "extreme measures",' said Sophia, coming over to us.

'Really?' I was surprised, but not really bothered about anything not absolutely directly concerning me right now. 'Sophia, be an angel and go with them? Make sure the doc comes back ASAP and that no one uses Joseph for a football if they do get him out?'

'Of course. I am happy to be "an angel" for you, even though we of the Grellor race do not believe in celestial myths.'

'Thank you,' I said as she hurried after the doctor and friends. 'Luckily for me, I know angels exist. And I'm just hoping that some celestial myth is watching over me right now...'

The cultists brought the doctor back; Sophia wasn't with them. He looked half-triumphant, half-annoyed. 'Did you do it?' I asked him eagerly. 'Did you get the code?'

He gave a curt nod. 'Yes. They're down there now. I was not permitted to accompany them.'

'Yippee!' I cheered, which looking back was rather insensitive of me. 'You know, normally Joseph gets on my nerves. Far too keen on schedules and time-keeping and what have you. But I don't think I've ever been quite so keen to see an inanimate object in my life.'

It was quite a while before Sophia returned. Cultists kept creeping up to the doors and trying to get in to see the miracle occurring, but Claire shooed them all away. I had the occasional panic about what was going to happen, but Dr Doom just assured me that once we established communications I wouldn't have anything to worry about. Every time I tried to ask him about what might happen if we didn't establish communications, he shushed me. I supposed he was trying not to worry me, but it didn't work. He clearly didn't want to talk about the potential upcoming operation, which wasn't exactly reassuring. I was wondering how on earth he intended to slice me open – would he use a sharpened toothbrush too?

I didn't hear Sophia come back, I was right in the middle of a scream. The first I knew about it was when a little silver ball came shooshing over my head. When I was able to speak again I said, 'Hello Joseph.'

'Greetings, Professor Summerfield. I understand that you require my assistance? Would you like to know your appointments for the day?'

'Oh, yes please,' I said, fascinated. I thought I knew what was happening. Morning: panic. Afternoon: be sliced up. Evening: try to stay alive.

He hummed for a moment. 'Take Wolsey to vet re. worming.' A pause. 'That concludes the reminders for today.'

I was silent for a moment. Then I said, calmly and evenly, 'That's all I've got on today, is it?'

Joseph gave a worried buzz. 'Er, yes, Professor.'

'So, and let me get this quite straight, what you're telling me is this: that not only am I trapped in an impenetrable

146

prison on a hostile world which has now been taken over by a gang of dangerous loonies; about to give birth with severe complications, no medical facilities and a doctor from the most evil regime in the galaxy – *no offence*; surrounded by people who want to take my baby away even if I survive; not only all of this, but you are telling me that because I am trapped here my beloved cat may get worms?'

'Er, I am sure Mr Braxiatel will make arrang–'

'I think that, possibly, Joseph, you failed to take note of the initial part of my speech. The bit about being trapped in prison and about to give birth.' I was still sounding very calm. You know, in the way a kettle gets quieter just before the bit where it comes to the boil and spurts steam all over the place. 'Joseph, do you remember how I had a cricket match at my wedding?'

'Yes, Professor Summerfield.'

'I am thinking of arranging another cricket match when I get out of here. You will be expected to attend.'

'Er… certainly, Professor. I am able to keep score and –'

'That, Joseph, will not be the capacity in which you will be attending this cricket match.'

(Agitated hum.)

'Now, I wonder if we could get back to the subject of how I am about to give birth.'

'Of course, Professor.' A pause. 'It's just that I already knew all about it. Your Grel friend with the large quantity of weapons had informed me on our way here.'

I turned my head. Sophia, over by the other bunk, tried to wave encouragingly. She didn't manage it very well due to having her arms full. 'Fact: I have recovered my dataxe!' she called.

'And that's not all you recovered!' I said, slightly taken aback. 'Is that a Tarfle Savaging-dagger I see before me?'

'Confirmation: that is correct! Fact: I have assembled much weaponry for our protection and the glory of the Grel! But I must deliver some of it to the members of the cult; this was part of our bargain.'

147

'Oh gosh,' I said. I would have asked more, but another contraction hit as she left. The pain was getting more extreme, more... concentrated. I'm not what you'd call a wimp. But knowing I was going through all this pain for nothing – that no baby was going to be pushed out at the end of it – that every second and every contraction was increasing the danger both to it and myself... well, by the end I was shedding real tears.

Claire said: 'We can't wait any longer. It's too dangerous. And now we have Joseph... Joseph, we have to carry out a caesarean section with no medical equipment. Can you monitor Benny's condition?'

'Of course.'

'The most important thing is to use this device to communicate with the outside world –' the doctor began, but Claire turned on him, baring her teeth. She was really quite formidable.

'There is no time,' she hissed. 'You will not leave Benny. Joseph, if he tries to leave... stop him.' Joseph beeped in acknowledgement.

And then Claire said, 'It's going to be very dangerous.' She was whispering, then, but boy oh boy, I heard it. Any shred of confidence I had left fell away.

'Claire,' I pleaded. 'I know this has to happen. I know I could die unless you do something. My baby could die. But I can't. I just can't. I need an anaesthetic. Something, anything...'

She gave me an agonised look. I'd swear there were tears in her eyes. 'There's no medical equipment in the place at all. If there was, the Wolf would have found it by now, believe me. The Aseks didn't exactly care about healing us in the normal run of things, did they?'

'Claire,' I said, 'you know how, in a previous life, I was an archaeologist? Well, you pick up little bits of history along the way. And one of the things I happen to know about is that before people discovered it was a good idea to inhale laughing gas, more people died from the shock of the operation than from their injuries.'

'I know,' Claire said. 'But the thing is… well, the thing is, that without the operation they'd have died anyway. And in hideous and prolonged agony, usually.'

'Ah yes,' I said, trying to pull myself together. 'I knew I was overlooking a vital part of the argument. Thank you for setting me straight.'

The doctor was considering us both. 'Logic dictates, however,' he began, still looking utterly furious at Claire's stubbornness – 'logic dictates that prior to the introduction of specific chemical anaesthetics, there must have been something that was used during operations…'

'Didn't you study this stuff? It's medicine!' I asked him.

'No,' he said. 'Did you study how they dug up fossils before someone invented the trowel?'

I admitted that I had little knowledge of either pre-trowel archaeology or pre-gas anaesthesia. I suspected that vast quantities of alcohol may have been involved though, probably in both. 'Joseph? Any information stored on ancient methods of pain relief?' I asked.

'Negative, professor.'

'Damn.'

'How about Sophia?' Claire suggested. 'She knows lots of things.'

'Good fact!' I said.

Sophia was hurriedly got. She now looked slightly less like an armoured porcupine, carrying only her dataxe. 'Sophia, tell me everything you know about everyday anaesthetics,' I gasped.

She looked overjoyed at the opportunity. 'Fact: ingestion of the substance "marshmallow" causes instant loss of consciousness in the Criath people of Taghost. The mineral "alsusy", found on –'

I raised a hand to stop her. 'Er, Sophia? Could you limit this to humans, please. Go back to the early history of Earth, for example.'

Her lecture barely slowed. 'Fact: substances distilled from

the everyday plants "hemp" and "poppy" were used throughout the history of Earth to dull pain and reduce consciousness. Additional fact: large quantities of beverages made from fermented vegetable juice mixed with water were often consumed before a surgical procedure –'

'Mmmm,' I murmured. 'Fermented vegetable juice…'

'– especially on board sea-going vessels, where the beverage "rum" was exceedingly popular. An unfortunate side effect of this treatment, however, was a tendency for the patient to vomit on recovery.'

'Ah,' I said.

'Further fact: for anaesthetics known in the vernacular as "local", those which paralyse a specific part of the body only, a solution of a substance obtained from the Earth plant "coca" was used, and this continued into the twentieth century…'

'Yes, yes, yes,' I said, waving my hands frustratedly. 'None of this is much help, is it? I can hardly get off my face in here, can I?'

'Can't you?' said Claire.

'Pardon?' I said. 'Have I wandered into a strange parallel prison dimension where you not only think drugs and alcohol are good, you think we're able to get hold of them?' And then I realised. 'The Terpsechians!'

'Yes!' Claire nodded.

'Reluctant interjection: we have nothing with which to barter,' put in Sophia.

'Oh yes we do,' I told her. 'We have the thing the cult want more than anything else in the world. Run and tell the Wolf what we're after, would you? And Sophia?'

'Yes?'

'Don't take no for an answer.'

She shook her head so determinedly that her mouth tentacles couldn't keep up, and scurried out of the room. Three contractions later she returned, leading a rather worried-looking Terpsechian. Terpsechians, in case I haven't mentioned it already, are extremely large people who bear a marked resemblance to walruses, with a hint of elephant. Each has a small, tapering trunk, giant tusklike teeth, and blue, rubbery skin. This particular Terpsechian, whose name I seemed to remember was Zim, was a lovely pale bright colour that a paint manufacturer would probably call 'duck egg'. I greeted her with a scream of pain, as another contraction juddered my body.

'Fact: the substance loses its potency very quickly,' I heard Sophia tell Claire and the doctor, 'therefore Zim thought it advisable to come along herself, in order for Benny to have a permanent supply.'

'Harro,' said a tooth-filled voice. 'I vill do my beft to help.'

'Aaaaaaaaaagh!' I said.

A long blue rubbery thing suddenly dangled itself over my face, making me scream again even as the contraction subsided. 'Aaaah!'

'Sovvy,' said Zim, removing her trunk. 'Vat I vill do if fif. I vill drip on to fif peef of fmock matevial, and vou vill breaf in ver fumes.'

I turned my head and watched her wrinkle her trunk right up, and then slowly drip a clear substance from the end of it on to a piece of material torn from a smock.

'Oh, it comes out of your trunk,' I said. 'I suppose that's almost a relief. For a while, I imagined it came out of your...' my eyes darted suggestively.

'Oh no,' said Zim. 'Vat's vere ve afid comef from.'

Ah. Another mystery solved.

Just then I heard new footsteps. Gripper. 'Heard you were about to go under,' she said. 'Thought I'd just pop in to say 'bye in case you don't...' she trailed off. 'Still, I can see you're busy. I'll be off.'

It did all look fairly industrious. Claire and Dr Doom were tying pieces of wet smock material around their faces. I suppose it wouldn't do if they were to get all giggly in the middle of the operation. Sophia appeared to have left the room again, but I suppose she wouldn't be needed during the operation. Hang on, the operation...

Zim passed the drug-soaked rag to Claire, who waved it under my nose. With the first heady whiff, I inhaled a bucket-load of calm. I almost forgot what I'd been about to shout about.

Oh yes. 'The operation...' I muttered to Claire. 'No equipment...'

I just had time to see the doctor holding up the Tarfle Savaging-Dagger before I drifted right away.

I have my eyes closed, and from the inside the lids look warm red in the sunlight. The sun has crept up through my body, warming the blood in my toes and watching the heat spread through my veins: feet, ankles, legs, the leg bone's connected to the thigh bone, the thigh bone's connected to the hip bone, the hip bone's connected to the shoulder bone, now hear the word of the Lord...

I love being outside. Outside is me. I am not an inside girl. Trees and grass and flowers are good. Me and the weather, we like each other. I love the sun and I love the rain and I even love the snow. Hail, admittedly, I can take or leave. But snow... I'm sticking my tongue out and the snowflakes are falling on it. I can't decide whether to eat them or let them melt first. In the end, I hold my head right back with my mouth wide open and they slip down without me having to do anything about it. I fall backwards on to the freezing crisp ground, blades of grass snapping with the weight of my body, each one the tiniest fraction of a second after the last so I can hear every single bone-fracture crack.

But the sun has melted all the snow.

I am lying on the sweet fresh grass. Slowly, oh so slowly, it grows around me. Questing stalks wavering between my fingers and my toes. A green silhouette springing up all around; creeping down my sides and up between my legs. My limbs glide from side to side, creating a grass angel. A shoot pushes its way through my stomach. I watch, intrigued, as life springs from me.

It's ripping me apart, and I can hear my mother calling me.

The grass is growing too high, too high above the ground. My angel opens and I sink into the earth. It closes above me. I am part of nature. Worms and beetles eat my flesh. Each nibble feels like a tickle and I'm laughing inside. My skin has gone and my bones are earth and I feel wonderful.

But the grass still grows through me. And it's getting thicker now. My mother's voice fades as my stomach splits from side to side and my skinless lips are screaming with the greatest pain I've ever known.

This stubborn shoot explodes through and from my nature and tears into the light. It bursts into flower: the most beautiful flower in the world. But I am still screaming.

'Benny. Benny, oh Benny, oh dear Benny, it's okay, it's all okay... Shh, my love, it's all right, I promise it's all right...'

The pain. The pain was still there. But little arms were holding me, a furry cheek was pressed against mine. Traces of a strong, sweet smell lingered in my nostrils and I sucked in air greedily, trying to get it back. That sweetness would take me away from the pain, I knew it would. But the sweetness had been taken away.

My eyelids flutter open, and Claire is there. 'Mm?' I manage.

I felt a tear splash on to my cheek, but it wasn't mine. 'Everything's all right,' she smiled through her sobs. 'Benny, you have a perfect baby boy.'

I couldn't quite take that in. I had a baby boy? How could that be possible? What was she talking about? And then my mental jigsaw began to reassemble itself. I struggled to sit up, crying out at the pain.

There was blood everywhere. Claire was covered in it, and from what I could see of myself, so was I. I was assuming it was all mine. I tenderly touched my deflated stomach, and felt a rough ridge snaking across it. Just the slightest brush of the fingers made me yelp. 'Joseph cauterised the wound,' Claire said. 'It's... well, when we get out of here, it'll be sorted properly.' I decided not to dwell on that. Zim the

Terpsechian was sat in a corner, seemingly unconscious. 'Fainted at the sight of blood,' Claire said, seeing the direction of my glance. I didn't blame her. Did I mention how much blood there was? Dr Doom was standing at the end of the bunk, his dark red uniform now even darker and redder. In one hand he was still holding the Tarfle Savaging-Dagger, its blade liquid-bright. In the other... in the other, in the crook of his arm, he was holding a reddy-pinky-yellowy thing. I focused, and saw a tiny creature. My son.

This is my son: he is perfect. Bloody, but perfect. He has huge black eyes and a nose like a kitten, and a shock of blond hair – fur? – on his head. His tiny chipolata fingers have tiny claws at their ends. His mouth is open, but it seems to be in wonderment – he's not crying. I have fallen in the deepest love possible.

The doctor moves forward. He is going to hand me my baby, to have and to hold. Movement from the other side of the cell: Sophia rushes in. She is gripping her dataxe in both hands. She runs towards the doctor, towards my baby, swinging the weapon wildly.

Claire is jumping up from my side, I am screaming 'Noooooooooooooo!' but it is too late as the dataxe swings.

I turn my head away, but still hear the thud.

15
New Life

Sophia stood in the middle of the cell, gasping. I tried to struggle out of the bunk, but Claire was already over there. She lifted my son out of the arms of the dead man, and handed him, wordlessly, to me. I cuddled him to my breast as I tried to make sense of it all. When you've become a mother and then seen the deliverer of your child killed in front of your eyes within seconds – well, I'm sure you'll understand that it's a lot to take in all at once.

'Why?' I asked, my eyes never leaving my baby. 'Were you working for the cult all this time, Sophia? A bit of a coincidence you arrived here the same day all the cultists did. A bit of a coincidence you told the Wolf about Jevina. A bit of a coincidence they let the doctor live on your say-so. A bit of a coincidence they let you get Joseph, and your dataxe, and drugs for me. A bit of a coincidence that you handed all those weapons over to them. So, what do you plan to do now?'

There was a pause, then Sophia spoke. 'Inference: you have, as the human saying has it, "got hold of the wrong end of the stick". I am not working for the cult. I have just killed the Fifth Axis Imperator, to prevent him from murdering your baby.'

'*What?*' I finally dragged my gaze from the beautiful little face. 'The… Fifth… Axis… Imperator…?'

'Fact: that is who he was.'

I opened and shut my mouth a few times, and finally said: 'Could you start back at the beginning, please?'

'Of course. Fact: In the beginning was Grellor. The Grel –'

'Not that far back,' I said hastily. 'Just the stuff about the Imperator. I mean, are you *sure* that was him? He seemed almost… nice.'

'Reassurance: that was indeed the Imperator. I received

155

that fact from Fifth Axis spy Gripper, and have since confirmed it.'

'But... but... what the hell was the Imperator of the Fifth Axis doing here in the first place? Why was he pretending to be a doctor?'

'Reluctant admission: I believe that to be my fault,' said Sophia, nervously.

'How?' I asked.

'Fact: it was I who, upon seeing the massacre of the Fifth Axis guards, asked if he were the doctor for you. Inadvertently I offered him an identity that would save him from the cultists.'

And I was thinking... our plan must have worked. Our ludicrous, half-baked, can't-think-of-anything-better plan must have actually worked! Gripper had passed on the information, and the Imperator had come to investigate! He couldn't trust his subordinates because of the lies we'd fed him, so he'd come himself! And that was why Straklant had been taken down to a holding cell. I wondered idly if the Imperator had had time to 'interrogate' Straklant before the cultists interrupted...

I shouldn't think like that, I know I shouldn't. I wish I didn't – I wish I were a better person. You see, I've been tortured, myself. Really tortured, the sort where you truly do long for death. Took me a long time to recover. It's the sort of thing which leads you to say: 'I wouldn't wish it on my worst enemy'. But I'm only human. My worst enemy was here, and I did wish it on him.

'I will now tell you the events leading up to this recent occurrence,' Sophia continued. 'Fact: when Gripper earlier entered the cell, I noted a look of extreme surprise and discomfiture cross her face. Curious as to the reasoning behind this, I followed her on her hasty exit, as she hurried towards the way out, only to observe her muttering the following words: "holy shit". I enquired of her the reason for this utterance, but she refused to give me an explanation. At that moment, a number of cultists, including Marianne, were clearing bodies in the dining room. Observing my pursuit, they exited and restrained Gripper before she could leave the floor. I told them of her suspicious behaviour, and they questioned her further. As she would not answer, they dragged her off to the Wolf.'

She paused. I glanced up at her; she was looking very uncomfortable. 'What is it?' I asked.

She shook her head. 'I am not going to tell you what then happened. All I will tell you is the following information, given by Gripper to the Wolf. As we were already aware, it is a fact that the Axis were aware all along of the Cultists' search for the baby of prophecy. They secretly provided the cultists with all manner of equipment to aid them in their search, until they found a child who would fulfil their conditions. This child was yours, Benny. Further equipment provided – unbeknownst to the cult – by the Fifth Axis, enabled them to drag your shuttle off course and bring it down on Deirbhile.'

'We know all this!' I interrupted. 'I mean, it still doesn't explain everything, and if you ask me it's a ridiculous effort to go to, and it doesn't explain how they happened to pick me in the first place, but...'

Sophia shrugged. 'It was the understanding of Gripper that anyone whose circumstances could be twisted to fit the terms of the prophecy would be adequate.'

'But how did they know about me in the first place? How did they know I was "adequate"?'

To my surprise, an electronic throat-clearance indicated that Joseph had something to contribute. 'What do you know about this?' I demanded, turning on him.

'It is rather a long tale, Professor Summerfield,' he began.

'Oh,' I said. 'Well, save it till Sophia's finished, then.'

At a nod, Sophia carried on with her extraordinary explanation. 'Fact: the cult had many ties off-planet, and the Fifth Axis had begun to regard them as a considerable danger. However they did not want to abandon Deirbhile as their strategic base; nor did they want to squander their resources on searching for cultists. Their plan therefore was this: to distract the cultists from active resistance by providing them with another focus for their activity, namely the search for the "child of two mothers". Then, when such a baby had been found, to kill it, thus destroying the cult's raison d'etre.'

'Kill it,' I said, numbly.

'Yes.'

'Not have it born under the noses of the Fifth Axis and prove that resistance is futile?'

'No.'

'Actually kill it.'

'Yes. That is why Gripper was placed in your cell. After the child was born, she was to wait until the cult had declared it to be their saviour, and then she was to kill it.' Sophia shot a glance at my baby. I followed her look.

My baby. They'd been going to kill my baby. This beautiful bundle of uncomplaining adorableness was supposed to have been sacrificed on the altar of the Fifth Axis. Would he have cried then? I wondered. Would he have cried when she took him away from me? Would he have cried when she put the dagger to his throat? Or would he just have kept looking up at her with deep, trusting onyx eyes?

I shivered.

Claire must have had an idea of how I was feeling, because she tried to break the spell. 'Er, Joseph, what was it you were going to explain?' she said. Hmm. She could possibly have chosen a better subject for a distraction.

Joseph hovered importantly. 'In accordance with your last instruction, Professor Summerfield, I have been monitoring all electronic data throughout the structure, and discov –'

'Hang on a minute. My "last instruction"?'

'To "keep my electronic ears open, you know, for electronic stuff".'

'Ah. That last instruction.'

'Indeed. Therefore, since our unfortunate landing on this planet, I have recorded all instances of electronic data that have come within my, ahem, "sphere" of influence.' Joseph wobbled slightly, obviously believing that he had been amusing. 'After I was placed in a most unpleasant room in the depths of this structure I was unable to monitor outside communications due to a dampening field. I did, however, find myself able to access stored data on several electronic items with which I shared temporary lodgings.'

'Confiscated datapads from other prisoners?' suggested Claire.

'Indeed. Amongst the recorded data I discovered the following, aspects of which correspond to one of my permanent voice-print records.'

Oh my gosh. This was it. I was going to discover who was the traitor; who had sold me out to these mad cultists. Which of my friends wasn't a friend at all.

Well, guess who it turned out to be.

There were two voices, one male, one female. The female had a soft, utterly feminine voice. I hated her already. So much so that I didn't actually work out who she was until half way through the recording. The male – well, the male voice I recognised straight away. I'd heard it in my dreams for months. And then, unfortunately, in real life again when I'd stupidly gone out of my way to rescue him...

MAN: Hi. Has anyone ever told you you'd be great in the movies?

WOMAN: Really?

MAN: Oh yeah. I'm actually a producer, you know. With that body, and that hair... Hey, why don't I buy you a drink and we can talk about it?

WOMAN: Well, I was sort of busy, but... yes, all right. That'd be nice.

MAN: Great!

WOMAN: So what sort of movies do you make?

MAN: Oh, plenty of time for all that. Let's get that drink. Barman! (a clink of glasses) Now, about your audition...

WOMAN: Audition?

MAN: Well, I mean, I like your look, but I have to check you can... take direction. That the camera likes you, that sort of thing.

WOMAN: I'm not sure...

MAN: Oh, it's okay. I'm a married man... well, sort of.

WOMAN: What do you mean, "sort of"?

MAN: Oh, you know how it goes, argue, divorce, get trapped in a demon dimension and she gets pregnant while you're gone – that sort of thing.

WOMAN: Gosh.

MAN: Yeah, and you'll never believe this, she says it's not even hers!

WOMAN: What do you mean?

MAN: Oh, nothing. Ignore me. Talking rubbish.

WOMAN: (very eager) Please, tell me what you meant!

MAN: Nothing. Really. Shouldn't talk about it. Look, let's forget about that drink. I've got to go.

WOMAN: No, please, come back...

(Click. Buzz. Click.)

WOMAN: Hi. Um, anyone sitting here?

MAN: No. I'm all on my own. All on my own, as usual.

WOMAN: Remember me?

MAN: Er...

WOMAN: A few days ago. Zita's Bar? You wanted me to audition for your film?

MAN: Oh. Right. Dunno if I'm going to make any more films. Whadderthey get me? Jus' money. Tha's all. Jus' money. Lotsa money. Piles o'the stuff. Whadder I wan' that for, huh? Mywife'sgotanotherman'sbaby.Why'dIwan'moneywhencan' haveBenny'n'baby?

WOMAN: You can't have them?

MAN: Nope. Not mine. Not want me.

WOMAN: So the baby's not yours, Mr Kane? And Bernice says it's not hers either? Could you tell me about that?

MAN: You've got pretty hair.

WOMAN: Thank you.

MAN: Wou' you like a drink?

WOMAN: You seem to have already had some!

MAN: Not nuff. Only... oooh, about twenty-seven. Big ones.

They don't make alcohol the way they used to. Stupid non-demonic dimension. Drink's s'posed to make you forget, innit? Well, it's making me remember even more.

WOMAN: Tell me about it.

MAN: You too, huh?

WOMAN: No, that wasn't a random expression of solidarity, I actually would like you to tell me about it.

MAN: Prob'ly wouldn't seem that bad to anyone else. After all, we were divorced. And I was in another dimension an' all.

WOMAN: Please. Tell me about it. And then perhaps we could go back to your place...?

And so he told her all about it. And, it seemed, took her back to his place. Or rather, my place. To the Braxiatel Collection, where she could keep tabs on me. Tamper with my shuttle. That sort of thing.

'I don't believe it!' I yelled, when Joseph finally stopped. 'Jason bloody Kane! I might have known! Spilling my secrets to some little cultist cow! Oh, they just have to wiggle their chests vaguely in his direction and he'll tell them anything they want to know! Secrets! He wouldn't know a secret if it bit him on his behind, and there's a lot of it there to bite these days let me tell you!' I decided to clarify that. 'I mean that he's running to fat, not that I've been biting his bottom. Well, not recently.'

   'The other voice sounded a bit familiar,' broke in Claire, sounding puzzled.

   'Oh yes,' I said. 'It did, didn't it. Do you know why? Do you know why it sounded familiar?'

   'Possibly because we've heard it before?' she ventured.

'Well, yes. We've heard it before, because it belongs to that drippy-dippy butter-wouldn't-melt Marianne! All "Great Mother" this and "Great Mother" that, and all the time she was really a bloody cultist!'

'To be fair, she's never actually pretended not to be a cultist,' Claire murmured, but I wasn't going to let little things like facts get in my way.

'And she's been sleeping with my husband!'

'Ex-husband,' muttered Claire. 'And we don't actually know...'

'You have *met* Jason, haven't you?' I said. 'I didn't call him "Mr Rabbit" because of his long floppy ears and twitchy nose.'

Claire seemed to shudder. 'I didn't know you called him "Mr Rabbit",' she said. 'In fact, I didn't want to know.'

'Oooooh,' I continued, 'if I wasn't currently totally unable to move due to having just had a baby and being in great pain, she'd know what it's like to face the wrath of Bernice Summerfield...'

I tried to sit up indignantly, but screamed involuntarily. Oh goddess, the pain!

Claire pushed me back gently. 'I know,' she said, softly. 'But as soon as we get out of here, to a proper doctor, they'll give you pain relief, sort everything out...'

'But how are we going to get out of here?' I sobbed. 'We're trapped in here. And that cult won't let me take my baby away!' I clutched him tighter to me.

Actually, I was amazed that the cult hadn't shown up earlier. Where were they, to greet their saviour? I tried to twist round, to see if there were any cultists out in the corridor, but just ended up screaming again.

'Fact: a large number of prisoners, including the cultists, are currently engaged in combat,' Sophia said, as if having read my mind.

'Combat?' queried Claire.

'Indeed: combat. Both hand to hand and involving the use of projectiles. I tried to inform them that the throwing of objects was against human law, but they would not listen! The introduction of weaponry has caused a great deal of conflict amongst prisoners. Many old grievances are being settled; also a number of new ones created since the fighting began. In addition: the mixture of male and female inmates is causing... incidents.'

'Incidents,' I stated. Sophia declined to elaborate, except to say: 'A lot of people are getting hurt.'

'Bet they don't hurt as much as me,' I muttered. I looked over at the now-snoring Zim. 'I don't suppose anyone would care to wake her up and get me another dose of happy juice?' I asked.

'I think we need all our wits about us...' Claire said, sounding agitated.

'Hang on a minute,' I said. 'What do you mean, throwing objects isn't against human law?'

Sophia bridled at this. 'Fact: you told me so yourself!' she said. 'It is stated by humans: those persons who live in buildings made of glass must not throw stones! This is a glass building, so they must not throw stones.'

'They're criminals, Sophia,' I said. 'They probably don't care.'

I looked down at my baby. His face seemed to be blurring. I worried for a moment that his strange birth had left him unstable. But, of course, it turned out to be me. All of a sudden I was very dizzy. I sighed, and almost dropped him.

Claire darted forward and took him from my unresisting arms. 'We need to get her to a doctor,' I heard her say.

'But the baby...?'

'The baby is fine. It's Benny who isn't.'

Too true. But at least my baby was fine. Nothing else really mattered. Their conversation continued like an out-of-tune radio in the background.

'We have to get a message out somehow. Joseph, could you break through the comms exclusion zone?'

'Er, no. I have attempted this. Unfortunately it's beyond my capabilities. Were I to be outside the exclusion zone,

I could communicate with the authorities, even, I believe, with the Braxiatel Collection, but in here, alas....'

'So there's no point even trying to fight through to the control systems. We don't know the top-security codes –'

'GOOD FACT!' Sophia's shout was so loud and so excited that I was jerked back into the room. 'Good fact: I have all the codes!'

'Er-um?' I asked, weakly.

'All the information possessed by the Fifth Axis Imperator is now stored in my dataxe! I have all the codes!'

Oh goddess.

Claire was squeaking her head off. 'We can get out! We can get out!'

'Um, save universe,' I muttered.

'And we can save the universe!' she squeaked even more loudly. 'Sophia, if you have access to *everything* the Imperator knew....'

'We will know all the plans of the Fifth Axis! We will know about their conference! We will know about their invasions! We will know the identity of every Axis member on every world! We can let everyone know! We can prevent them taking over the galaxy!'

Everything was going to be okay. I didn't want to die, but even if I did, everything was going to be okay. The voices gradually faded away...

A cupful of cold water hit my face. 'Benny, wake up, wake up, please!'

I opened my eyes. The room was darker than I remembered it. Sophia had gone, so had Joseph, so had Zim the sleeping Terpsechian. There was just Claire. And my baby. Claire was pressing him against my wet cheek.

'Ever'thing okay now...' I whispered. 'No war... no slaughter...'

Claire nodded. 'Sophia and Joseph have gone down to A floor,' she said. 'Joseph will access the data from Sophia's dataxe, and use the codes to open the main doors. Then they're going to get outside the exclusion zone and transmit everything they know to the entire galaxy.' She paused. 'And tell Brax where we are. And get a doctor.'

'Too late,' I muttered.

'No!' Claire sounded angry. She had no right to be angry. I was dying. Not allowed to be angry with dying people. 'You mustn't give up, not now! The galaxy's saved, and that's all well and good, but you have to be a mother now. You told me yourself. You didn't want your baby to grow up without a mother.'

She took hold of my right hand, and lifted it up to stroke my baby's silky hair.

Something coursed through me like static electricity. I tingled all over.

'He's going to have his mother,' I said. Claire hugged me tight. It hurt.

We lay there on the bunk, Claire, baby and I. The cultists had left us alone – they obviously had other battles to fight, but even though the cell door was open, we couldn't hear anything. It was so still and silent. Occasionally my baby made a slight gurgling hiccup as he moved, but there was no other sound.

My baby had been so quiet the whole time. Gurgles and stuff, but no crying. I thought all babies cried, but obviously not. 'It's not necessarily a bad sign,' Claire said. 'He's half-Killoran, after all. They're tough. When was the last time you heard Adrian Wall cry?'

'He yells a lot,' I pointed out. 'Does that count?'

She giggled. 'Really, Benny, he seems completely healthy. I don't think you need to worry about it.'

'How will I know when he's hungry if he doesn't cry?' I said. 'For that matter, how do I feed him? Will he just know what to do?'

Claire giggled again. 'Yes, yes, he'll know what to do. But it's you who needs feeding up right now. I'm going to go to see if I can get hold of some nutrition blocks. You have to keep your strength up, it's very important at the moment.'

She hopped off the bed and trotted to the door. As she reached the doorway, she turned back for a second. 'You're not a quitter, Benny. Don't give up again while I'm gone.'

I wasn't going to give up. But… but sometimes it's not about giving up. Sometimes fighting just isn't enough. Letting go isn't about cowardice; sometimes it just happens. I've known so many brave and beautiful people who have died. They didn't 'give up'.

I didn't think I could bear to leave my baby. But I had a feeling I would have no choice in the matter.

'I'm sorry, little one,' I whispered to the dozing bundle in my arms. 'I don't think we're both going to make it. But whatever happens, you'll always be loved. Claire, or Adrian, or Brax, or Jason, they'll take care of you. And maybe, one day, they'll explain to you about your mother. About how she loved you so much. And she wanted to be there for you always, but she just couldn't. Like my mother couldn't be there for me. It doesn't mean she stopped loving me. And I will never, ever stop loving you.'

He turned over again, and I lay there with his hot breath hitting my cheek.

I had almost fallen asleep when Claire came bursting in in a state of sheer panic. It took a few seconds for me to make out what she was saying. 'Straklant! Straklant! This way!'

'Calm down,' I told her, feeling anything but calm myself. 'You've seen Straklant?'

She gulped in air, eyes closed. For a second I thought she was going to faint. 'It's Straklant,' she said when she had the breath. 'All the doors have opened – Sophia and Joseph must have opened them all – let him out. I saw him, he's got as far as C floor, but he must be coming here and he's not alone… oh Benny, I'm scared.'

I glanced down at baby. His eyes flickered open, and he gazed back up with trusting eyes. This isn't how it was meant to be. It was supposed to be all over. Story's end. My baby was supposed to ride off into the sunset, safe.

I tried to struggle upright. Oh goddess, the pain was so bad. There were tears in my eyes. 'I can't make it!' I screamed. 'I can't make it! He'll find us! He'll kill my baby!'

'No, no,' Claire cried, 'we won't let him, we won't!'

'Shut the door!' I cried, desperate. 'There must be a way to shut the door!'

'I can't, Benny,' she sobbed, 'you know I can't! It's all controlled centrally! We need the codes, we need Joseph…'

I thrust baby at her. 'Then take him!' I implored her. 'Take him. Run. Go outside, find Sophia and Joseph. Get out of here.'

'I'm not leaving you!'

'Yes, you are. Get out of the prison. Get hold of Brax. Make sure all the information gets out. And just… keep him safe. Now *go*!' I screamed.

She gave me an anguished look, but grabbed my darling, uncomplaining child and ran out without a backward glance. 'I love you,' I muttered. 'I love you, and I never even told you your name.'

I managed to get myself on to the floor – I don't know why, I knew I couldn't get away, but lying back and waiting – that was something that I just couldn't do.

I crawled towards the door on my hands and knees. Every shuffling step was an agony, white hot knitting needles piercing my stomach. And then like a knife wound, so intense that it took my breath away and my scream twisted in my throat. The floor below me was spotted with red, and I imagined the fused line that circled my stomach ripping and tearing. In my head, I knew that was all that was holding me together. The wound would burst, and my body would lay in two halves on the floor like I was a Russian doll.

I was already weak from all the blood I'd lost. I couldn't lose any more. Stupidly, I tried to scrape up the drops from the floor, some barely lucid idea of feeding it back inside my stomach. I needed it all. Couldn't afford to lose any.

The bit of my mind that was still in the real world knew what was happening.

I would have died anyway. I knew that from the things Claire didn't say. The blood loss. The high risk of infection. The lack of drugs. The improbability of getting treatment in time. Everything. I knew it even more from how I felt. The birth had not felt like a beginning for me, it had felt like an ending. I wasn't giving up. But I knew I was going to die.

And then Straklant walked in. I managed to focus on his shoes. There were other shoes behind him, and with a huge effort I turned my head far enough to see who his companion was: Crow.

I almost felt a brief moment of satisfaction. 'I *knew* it was you!' I whispered to the woman. There was sheer terror in my breast, but somehow I felt I had to keep talking. Not let him see that he'd won. Even though he had. And of course he could see it.

'Oh, well done,' said Straklant. 'Clever Professor Summerfield.'

'But… why?' I was dying. It didn't mean I wasn't curious. And I had to keep him talking. Keep him occupied. Let Claire and my son get as far away from him as possible. 'What could you offer her to make it worthwhile?'

He smiled at that. 'Gratification,' he said.

'Sex?' I whispered. 'Chocolate?' I pulled myself together as best I could. 'A really thick milkshake with… whipped cream on the top and a couple of… bendy straws?'

'No,' he said, putting his stump round her neck and considering her like she was a star pupil, 'she just likes to hurt people. After all, Benny, this is a prison. It was fairly easy to find someone who enjoys being – hmm, how shall I put it? – a bit naughty. I did so laugh to hear about your detective work. There was no motive. There was no grand plan. It was so much simpler than that.'

You've really been to villain school since I last saw you, I thought. You've got the immoral silent sidekick, and now you're gloating.

He lifted an eyebrow. 'Tell me, didn't you ever wonder why you were still alive?'

I sniffed at him. 'Because you're incompetent and I'm… quite clever?'

'No.' Bugger. 'Because Crow wasn't trying to kill you. Not

that she didn't want to –' he smiled at her indulgently – 'but I was always intending to take care of that personally. I just wanted you terrorised and hurt. I want you to suffer before I kill you, suffer like I have.'

Suffer like he has? Oh boy. That got me so mad I was up on one elbow without even noticing the effort. Adrenaline hit me through my anger. 'Oh, I'm *so* sorry you got put into prison after killing lots of nice people for no good reason. Boy, your suffering is huge compared to theirs.'

'That's not why I got put in here, and you know it. You set me up!'

I nodded. 'True. But it doesn't actually mean you… didn't commit all those crimes. You weren't going to be brought to justice in the normal way, so we… took a bit of a liberty. The end, I very firmly believe, justified the means. So your petty… revenge is meaningless.'

'*Petty* revenge? You ruined my life.'

'*I* ruined your life?' I was shaking now, and couldn't see him properly, but if my last words couldn't be of love for my son, then they were going to tell Straklant exactly what I thought of him, with every scrap of energy I had left. 'You know, it always amazes me how you evil guys swan around, being evil, evilly betraying everyone, destroying people who get in your way, and then blame other people if someone takes exception to it. You're hanging around with guys who are untrustworthy murderous bastards, and act surprised if they stop trusting you. Not my fault! Yours! You can't be the bad guy and expect other people to treat you nice. You do bad things, you hang out with bad people, you get a bad life. Deal with it.' I fell back on to the floor.

'No,' he said. 'I'm just going to sit on this bunk here and watch you die.' He looked up sharply. 'But before you do, I'm going to kill your baby.'

'Can't,' I whispered, all strength exhausted by my final outburst. 'Gone. You'll not get him.'

But I heard, as if very far away, yells and footfalls. 'I'm sorry, Benny.' I heard Claire's sobs through the haze. 'I'm so sorry. They caught me.' Then I think she must have seen me; her voice got closer. I felt tears falling on to my upturned eyelids. 'Benny, don't! Benny, wake up, please wake up! Stay with us, you must, oh you must!'

'Bring her round.' That was Straklant's voice, sounding urgent. 'She has to see this before she dies! I want her to suffer!'

I knew he was going to kill my baby. How could I suffer more, whether I witnessed it or died first?

'Joseph,' Claire sobbed. 'Benny's porter Joseph. He's down on A Floor. He can reseal the wound.'

But that won't help, I thought at her. It's too late.

16
He's Behind You!

There are torturers, they say, who can keep a person on the very point of death, in exquisite pain, for decades.

I guess they don't have much of a social life. Or many friends.

My porter Joseph must be one of them.

I don't want to die, I don't. I don't want to leave this life and all those I love, although – who knows? – I might see once again all those I have loved who have gone before me. But how can I accept that there is really something better out there, because why then would I have any reason to fight to keep my loved ones in this hell?

I don't think I can stand the pain much longer. I'm aware of little but the pain. It consumes you, burrows right into your core. Joseph is humming around me, concerned, but pleased he has stayed my execution, I can tell. Not for long, I beam towards him telepathically (not that we share any mental bond, just that I don't have the energy to speak). Not for long. You've just brought me back for more suffering. I don't blame you, but that's what you've done.

I can see Straklant's shoes. I'm getting to know them quite well. One thing about this place: we get to keep our own shoes, unless they're stiletto heels or full of nails or otherwise a potential weapon. Straklant's shoes are shiny. He's been in prison for months, and his shoes are still shiny. I believe this to be the mark of a true sociopath.

It's very, very quiet. I raise my head. As the dizziness passes, I realise that the cell door is shut, sealing us into this soundproof tomb. Claire is huddled in the far corner, my baby clutched desperately to her furry bosom. Joseph is hovering just out of reach of Straklant, who is standing a few feet away from me, his hands on his hips. I remember when I first met him, he was sweet, personable, attractive. Now he's a pantomime villain. Doesn't he realise that the longer one tortures and gloats, the more chance there is that one's victim will be rescued? Or perhaps he just doesn't care. Because to him, it's the torture and the gloating that's the important bit.

And we're not going to be rescued.

Propped up on my elbows now, and I could see that there was a commotion outside. Like watching a violent holovid with the sound turned off. I could see the Wolf, and Marianne, and all the others of the cult; they were hammering at the cell door, mouthing threats – to Straklant, not to me – and brandishing the largest variety of weapons I'd ever seen.

'Your ball closed the door for me,' said Straklant. I hadn't even begun to wonder how he'd managed it, but yes of course, Joseph knew all the codes now. 'I didn't want any interruptions.'

I glanced back at the front wall. I'd welcome any interruption right now, even from that bunch of loony baby-worshippers. 'Joseph, open the door again,' I gasped.

There was a distressed hum, as my little porter zoomed down to me. 'I can't!' he squeaked. 'The gentleman made me configure it to his voice print!'

'Then... break the door down! Use your laser beam!'

Straklant, assured I was conscious, was moving over towards Claire.

'Benny, I don't have a laser beam...'

'Glass shatters! Sing at it!'

I tried to pull myself up further. Claire was a little dynamo – hitting, biting, kicking Straklant. I don't think he had expected that.

'This door is not made of glass! It's all a question of finding the correct harmonic frequency at which this material will vibrate, and –'

'Find it! Find it!'

Outside the cell, Sophia had appeared, a nervous, skinny woman alongside her, dressed in Fifth Axis red. She was carrying what looked suspiciously like a medical bag.

'It is likely to be below the human range and therefore my own...'

'Just try!'

My ears began to hum with sound, my mind buzzing as I tried to crawl towards Straklant and Claire. Her teeth were locked into his arm, but it wasn't enough. He reached out for my baby...

'It's no good, Benny. I cannot produce the required frequency...'

Straklant grabbed my child.

And my baby cried for the very first time.

Can you imagine a growl crossed with a scream? That's the sound that a half-Killoran, half-human baby makes.

And below me, the floor began to vibrate.

The tiniest vibration. Barely noticeable. In fact, almost certainly unnoticeable to anyone who wasn't on their hands and knees on top of it. But definitely a vibration.

'Joseph!' I screamed. 'That's it! Quick! Record it! Amplify it!'

By a miracle, he got what I meant immediately. The cry filled up the cell as Joseph recorded and amplified and directed it at the door. And it actually worked. Hairline cracks began to appear. The thumps of the cultists shook shattering fragments to the floor. And as Straklant held my baby aloft, the Wolf and all the others burst through the door.

I saw the Wolf grab my baby.

And I passed out again.

17
The Awakening

I seem to be waking up a lot recently. More than the average once per day, that is. But for the first awakening in what seemed like for ever, I woke up happy. There was still pain, but it was dull and far away, and you know what? I didn't think I was about to die. I suddenly remembered how to smile.

But you know that classic bit that comes just after, when you remember all the bad things and jerk into full consciousness? Yes, that's right.

I opened my eyes, and saw a Grel standing over me wielding a brain-stained dataxe. I yelped, until things clicked into gear and I realised it was Sophia. The dataxe was slung casually in the direction, not of me, but of the skinny woman I'd seen earlier.

'Fact: Benny is awake!' Sophia called out over her shoulder.

'So can I go now?' demanded the skinny woman, who had her arms crossed firmly in what I recognised as an extremely defensive pose.

'Query: have you done all you can for Benny?'

The woman looked irritated. 'I'm a doctor. Of course I have.'

'My baby!' I gasped.

Sophia shushed me. 'Fact... he is safe,' she said, turning back to the woman. 'Doctor?'

'Yes, I've done everything I can. I've stabilised her, but she's still extremely weak. Shock and blood loss, mainly, but she needs to rest for at least a week, probably a lot longer. I've also given her something to stave off the risk of infection. The... wound, however, could reopen with strenuous activity, and must be properly treated in a hospital. But as I'm not a hospital, I'll be going now.'

She spun on her heel and exited briskly. Sophia didn't try

to stop her.

'Was she Fifth Axis?' I said.

Sophia nodded.

'And you're just letting her go?'

'There is no point in stopping her. Unfortunate fact: the soldiers of the Fifth Axis are overrunning this prison.'

So a few things had been happening while I was out of it. I wanted to know all about them. But first... 'My baby – you're sure he's safe?'

She looked extremely uncomfortable. 'Grel do not lie!'

'But they can bend the truth... Tell me what's happened, Sophia!'

She hung her head. 'Fact: your baby is indeed safe, in that no harm has come to him. However...'

'Sophia!' I cried, trying to pull myself up (it hurt).

'He is with the cult. But he is safe!'

A wave of dizziness and nausea flowed over me. I collapsed back on the pillow and shut my eyes – I couldn't move. 'Tell me what happened,' I croaked.

She told me. She and Joseph had gone down to A floor, armed with all the information from (and I got very slightly squeamish at this point) the Imperator's brain. Which meant, as I knew, that they knew how to turn off the security systems, and gain access to all the door codes. To save time on working out which ones controlled the external doors, Joseph used the main override to open every door in the place. To cut a longish story short, as the Fifth Axis forces rushed in, Sophia smuggled herself out, and as soon as they were outside the communications exclusion zone Joseph sent out a general alert. Everyone in the galaxy knows about the Axis plans now.

So few words for such an enormous thing! I tried to express that to Sophia. The lives she'd saved! She blushed, and hurried on with her explanations. It was as they were coming back to the prison that she'd seen the woman – the tall, skinny woman in Fifth Axis red, standing and watching the troops as they took back the building. A little remote search of the security systems revealed that this was the doctor who had been expected in the first place. So Sophia and Joseph decided she should keep her appointment…

They came back in – the Axis troops being less concerned with people trying to break *into* prison – at which point Marianne had yelled at them from over the heads of the Axis soldiers guarding the staircase that she needed Joseph to save my life and Joseph had hovered over to her and vanished up the stairs. By the time Sophia had managed to sneak – and fight – her way to D floor, it was all happening. She stumbled over her words a bit then. After a bit of prodding, she confessed that it was her fault that Straklant had been released. She hadn't thought that opening the doors would let him out too… I could never forgive her. She would never forgive herself. I told her not to be so silly. It had all turned out all right in the end. Hadn't it?

What had happened to my baby?

When Joseph shattered the door, the cult had rushed in to the rescue. The rescue of the 'Great Mother' and the prophesied child, not Benny and her son, but the results were the same of course. They seized baby and Straklant. But Claire went with them, Sophia assured me, to make sure everything was all right…

Claire, fierce, loyal and lovely as she is, much as she'd shown her willingness to bite, versus the newly-armed cultists. I was less than comforted.

I struggled upright again. 'Come on,' I said. 'We've got to find them.'

I managed to pull myself on to the edge of the bed. Sophia was fussing around. 'The doctor said you had to rest! She said the wound could reopen!'

'I'm okay!' I insisted. It was a lie, but…

I managed to stand upright. I managed to take a step forward.

I managed to collapse flat on the floor.

'Fact: you are too ill to move! You must return to bed!'

'I'm fine. It's just that I still appear to have a pot-bellied pig attached to my waist. Moving is a slight problem, that's all. But if you help me...'

I held out my hands, and Sophia, with considerable effort, dragged me up. I leaned on her shoulder and looked around. 'There,' I said. There was a considerable amount of blue in the distance, and I would estimate that it was in the dining room. 'That's where they all are. Come on, Sophia. Best foot forward.'

'Fact: my feet are of equal worth to me...' Sophia began, as we staggered out of the cell. I'm not sure how long it took us to get to the dining hall. They spotted us before we got there, and Claire and several cultists came out to help. I was carried into the room, but as we reached the door and I could clearly see my beautiful, once-more silent son, I broke away and managed to stumble towards him, arms stretched forward like a sleepwalker. I think the Wolf was so stunned to see me (a) alive and (b) walking that she didn't quite realise what she was doing as she surrendered baby to me.

'Well... you're just in time,' she told me. 'You wouldn't want to miss this.'

We were still in the dining hall. Joseph, on request – or, I should say, in response to threats, and not from me – had locked the door. Occasionally we saw a Fifth Axis trooper or a prisoner run past, but as we could see through the floor most of the combat was raging on below us. Most of the prisoners had made it down to A floor before the troops arrived, and although some of them had fled back upwards, the battle proper was down there. Now there were Fifth Axis soldiers stationed at the only exit from the upper floors, to stop anyone else fleeing upwards, and to catch anyone else who came down. The prisoners wanted to leave, and the troops wanted to stop them leaving. Those were the simple facts of it, but it happened to translate into a life-or-death struggle.

Joseph had also reprogrammed the food dispenser – not so that it produced anything other than the cardboard muck, unfortunately, but at least you could have as much of the disgusting stuff as you wanted. It is a tribute to how hungry we prisoners were kept that almost everyone availed themselves of this dubious service.

It was just like going to the circus. Load yourself up with snacks, and then settle down to watch the show. In this case, the kangaroo trial of Kolonel Daglan Straklant; resident judge: the Wolf.

It was almost laughable. Down there: chaos. In this one, isolated room, the pretence of organised justice being done. The Wolf was standing on a bench over the far side of the room, the rest of the Cultists sitting on benches nearby. Straklant was tied to the water dispenser with blanket strips. Sophia and Claire had helped me to a bench as far away from everyone else and – at my insistence – as near to the door as possible. Apart from us, the only other non-cultist present was our one-time next door neighbour, lizard-skinned Thall. She leant against the wall a few feet away from us, eyes half closed, seemingly uninterested in what was going on.

The Wolf had tried to take back my baby, but had soon realised that in my current… excitable, shall we say? state, and with an already battle-hardened Grel with dataxe in hand by my side, it was not a good idea to attempt this. She contented herself with telling me I could remain custodian of their child for the time being.

There where points were I wasn't sure who I hated most, her or Straklant.

Unfortunately she'd also positioned a couple of cultist goons by the doorway: cultist goons with weapons. Which made my cunning plan of getting Joseph to unlock the doors so the four of us could get out rather redundant for now.

It was just all… ridiculous! I'd created life, I'd come *this* close to death, and now I was supposed to care about a bunch of stupid women prancing about pretending to be important while outside the galaxy could be falling. And even if their minds couldn't stretch that far, then here, here in this very place, the possibility of freedom was close at hand. There was chaos out there! If I were them, I'd be taking any chance to get out of here, planning a way to get past the guards, not sticking around waiting for the Axis to regain control and keep me inside for another dozen years! Break for freedom! You might get killed, but at least you might get the chance to taste fresh air again before you died. What good was a life in this place?

But no. Pretend to be in charge. Pretend this is in some way worthwhile. I won't pretend I didn't want revenge on Straklant. But I wanted freedom more!

The Wolf was yelling from her bench. 'This is the man who tried to kill the prophesied child, our saviour!'

There were boos from her audience. I resisted the temptation to shout out: 'Oh no it isn't!' But only because, well, they happened to be right.

'Is it just Straklant on trial?' I whispered to Claire. 'What about Crow?'

Her eyes darted towards the slouching figure of Thall. 'You missed that,' she said softly. 'She's not a problem any more.'

'This man must face justice!' cried the Wolf.

'Kill him!' called someone.

'Hang him!' cried another.

'Make him suffer!' was a third cry. All good suggestions, I thought. Others I could think of involved boiling oil, cheese graters, and his private parts.

'We will administer justice,' the Wolf said. 'For threatening the life of our baby, he should die. But I have been reminded –' and here she glanced at her nearby lieutenant, Marianne (who wasn't going to persuade me she was Little Miss Innocent by that sort of thing, oh no) – 'that, by ancient law, the final decision should be made by the Great Mother, as he intended to take her life also. And she may administer whatever punishment she desires.'

All heads turned towards me.

What?

'You decide whether he should live or die. And in what manner.'

Well, bugger that for a game of soldiers.

'No way!' I said. 'Not my thing. This is your show; you don't absolve yourself of responsibility that easily.'

'Don't you want him dead? Don't you want him to suffer?'

Of course I did! But there's a difference between wanting the boiling oil and throwing the boiling oil, and an even greater difference between that and sitting patiently heating it up in the first place. 'Look, do whatever you like to him,' I said. 'Just don't... don't let him go.'

The Wolf shook her head. 'Ancient law,' she said. 'If you don't pronounce... then we will have to let him go.'

The cow. She was really enjoying this. I bet she and her husband-stealing chum had made up this 'ancient law' just to put me on the spot. I wanted the ground to open up and swallow the lot of them, Straklant and all.

And it did.

It was Joseph who first alerted me. 'Benny... I am detecting vibrations –' he began, seconds before the first crack jagged across the floor.

'What the –?' I cried.

'I fear the earlier vibrations are still resonating through the building,' Joseph said, a little shamefacedly (not that he had a face, but, well, vocabulary only goes so far). 'The whole structure has been... weakened.'

'You mean it's about to come down around our ears?!' I hissed at him. He bobbed up and down in guilty agreement.

'We've got to get out of here!' I said, shifting baby to the crook of one arm so I could grab hold of Claire with the other. She started to help me up, but one of the goons made a threatening gesture towards us.

'We've *all* got to get out of here!' I yelled to the room at large. 'It's unstable!' I gestured wildly at the increasing crack approaching from the far side of the room. 'Joseph, we're sixty feet up! Quick, open the door!' And then with the loudest, ugliest snap in the world, the floor collapsed completely. That was the last I ever saw of the Wolf,

Marianne, and the other cultists. Even the door-guarding goons were gone, not having had anything to cling on to.

We didn't fall, I should probably point that out. Sheer luck. The building was obviously weakest in the centre, the cracks radiating out from D20, where it had all begun. Wanting to be near the door, we'd just been the furthest ones away, while the Wolf, on the opposite side of the room, had been the nearest. We still had a jagged bit of floor to stand on, and were grabbing hold of our bench as tightly as we could. Thall, too, had not fallen, although she did not look as nonchalant now as she had done earlier.

Oh yes, and there was one other person left.

Attached to the water dispenser, that was attached to the wall, Kolonel Daglan Straklant was dangling over the gaping hole, held up by nothing more than a few threads of blanket.

He looked at me. It wasn't pleading, it wasn't anything really.

There was a ledge of glass round his side of the room and ours. We could reach him. The blanket bonds wouldn't hold him for long, but it would be long enough for one of us to get there and back.

What do you think? That I should have gone to him. Pulled him up. Demonstrated that I was the better person. Letting him fall would mean that I was as bad as he was.

Well, sod you. It wasn't your baby he was going to kill.

18
Through the Looking-Glass, and What I Found There

The cracks chased us down the stairs. I remembered a drunken midnight skating jaunt on the ornamental lake back on the Braxiatel Collection. I could have died then, too, but managed to get back to the lakeside before the ice fissures caught up with me. Now we had to be faster than the glass. Claire carried my baby, Sophia and Thall carried me. Crystal walls were crumbling from the inside, fracturing like shattered mirrors. The soldiers guarding the stairs had gone, and by the time we reached the bottom the stairs themselves had gone too. There were no entrances or exits, no doors or archways left.

We staggered out of the building, clambering over fallen lumps of glass, ducking from those that were still falling, and stepping in the rainbows that were here, there and everywhere as the sun shot through the pieces. Other prisoners, both males and females, were fleeing all around us, but in the depths of the wreckage that we were climbing over, flashes of blue and red – prisoners and Fifth Axis – could just about be made out. I did that, I thought. They are all dead because of me. But the sun was shining so brightly and I had my friends and my child. Later, it would come back to haunt me, but now I just basked in being free.

It would be nice to say that as we stumbled through the rubble, we looked up and saw a craft swooping towards us, ready to take us to freedom, but actually it was over four hours later that the ship turned up. By then the collapse was complete.

What did we do for those four hours? You know, I couldn't

tell you exactly, but I'll try my best. I do know that the first thing we did was run. Sophia and Thall lifted me off the ground and bore me away, Claire's little legs pounding as hard as they could to keep up until I had to ask my bearers to slow down so I could keep my baby in view. The prison didn't suddenly fall as soon as we were out of it, but kept going slowly, piece by piece, until there was nothing left but a pile of glittering rubble.

After it was all over, as we watched it from a safe distance, I thought: I did that, too.

I've replayed it a hundred times in my mind now. Sometimes my brain puts it in reverse, like in those humorous holovids of demolitions, and I see the building building up, bit by shining bit. As it solidifies, faces appear at the windows again, screaming.

We didn't know what to do or where to go. Someone – it must have been Thall, now I come to think about it – knew a place nearby that was fairly secluded, and we went there and tried to hide out. But having dispensed with her burden (me), Thall herself departed for a destination unknown. I was pleased to see her go. That sounds awful. But in the absence of being able to curl up in a small ball on my own, the next best thing was to be only with people I felt close to. And at the moment, that was Claire, Sophia and my baby.

No one said anything for quite a while. We were in a little hut; bare wooden floor and walls, but it was wonderful. No one was looking at us. No one could see in. It seemed the most perfect place in the whole world. I crept into a corner, relishing the sensation of my back against the solidity. I loved the fact that there was no view, no sunlight. I loved the fact that there was earth beneath my feet and I couldn't fall. And then the thing happened that made it even more perfect.

'Beep!' said Joseph.

I frowned at him. 'Did you just say "Beep"?'

'Er, yes,' he replied.

'Why?' I asked.

'It's in the manual,' he said. 'I'm supposed to beep when I intercept an incoming message.'

'Yes,' I said, 'you're supposed to beep, not *say* "Beep". Oh, never mind that now. You've intercepted an incoming message, then, have you?' And then I realised what that could mean. 'Joseph! The message the message the message! Give me!'

Joseph cleared his non-existent throat, and suddenly Irving Braxiatel's voice came out of his mouth. 'Benny. I hope you get this. We're on our way. Repeat: we're on our way. Message from Joseph received. Information passed out to all governments. Galaxy on full alert. And we're coming to take you home. Get Joseph to transmit a signal for us to home in on, otherwise we'll land and search for you on foot. Computer: repeat message until it's picked up.'

I'd polkaed halfway around the shed before I remembered my legs weren't working. Claire fussed over me for about quarter of an hour before she was satisfied I hadn't done myself any (more) permanent damage. But she was just as excited as me.

We were going home. And we'd saved the world.

Joseph beamed out a signal for Brax, and then managed to tune in to the Fifth Axis communication frequencies. We huddled in the shed, listening to the increasingly frantic transmissions. I remember cheering when we overheard that the conference was off. Then we heard that all planned military offensives had been abandoned. The death of the Imperator had caused chaos, but wasn't the worst thing. Some terrible person had been spreading rumours. Rumours that there was a traitor in the high ranks of the Axis. That Daglan Straklant had known who it was. That the Imperator had been lured to his death; and Straklant had been killed too to stop him telling what he knew. We intercepted private channels: 'I have it on good authority that Randolph is the traitor. Remember how he acted after Tranmar Bridge?'

'I've never trusted Timentis. Get the troops over to his

office. Make some excuse.'

And so it went on, the panic and suspicion escalating as the hours passed. Reports came in of assassinations, of attacks and ambushes. Of men revolting and killing their superior officers. Of soldiers running and changing sides. Of officers fleeing off-planet, only to be shot down. Of the upper echelons desperately calling upon their troops for protection, only to find they'd all been sent to the Glass Prison – and we knew from first-hand experience that there wouldn't be many left to respond to the calls.

We tried not to get too excited. I didn't resurrect any more ancient dance steps. It was early hours after all: Rome wasn't built in a day, and certainly didn't fall in a day either. But how could we resist rejoicing? For now, at least, the evil was impotent. Yes, more troops would be summoned. Yes, surviving officers would resurface, raise their forces, make new plans. But perhaps – just perhaps – this time the rest of us would be ready for them.

And that's just about all I remember, except for a fragment of conversation. It was just after we'd heard about the cessation of hostilities. 'Unbelievable fact: it is over,' Sophia said. 'The Glass Prison has fallen, and the Fifth Axis has also fallen.'

After a few seconds, Claire said: 'And you know who we have to thank.'

I tried to look modest. 'Well, all in a day's –'

'Your baby,' she continued. 'The cult was right. He brought us all together; he provided the impetus and ultimately the means of destruction.'

'Oh,' I said.

'It's just... it's a bit too much of a coincidence, isn't it? Your baby was supposed to destroy the Fifth Axis, and the Fifth Axis has been destroyed. His cry was at the very frequency that vibrated the prison. I don't know what the chances of that are –'

'I can easily work that out,' interrupted Joseph. 'Needless

to say, the odds are astronomical...'

'Oh, shut up, Joseph,' I said diplomatically.

'But Benny,' Claire went on, 'don't you think... Do you think... do you think the prophecy was real?'

'No I do not!' I said. 'Prophecies are bollocks! You can't have "too much" of a coincidence, in a way all coincidences are "too much" or we wouldn't notice them. But they happen.'

There was another thoughtful pause. 'Accepting that...' Claire began, with a mischievous smile, 'you once said that the only way prophecies could be "true" was if a time traveller had gone back into the past and given too much away. Well... you've travelled in time a lot, Benny.'

I wasn't entirely sure I liked where this was going. 'And?'

'And supposing one day in the future you just happen to pop back to ancient Deirbhile, knock back a bit too much of the local vodka, and start telling everyone how you're a *great mother*...'

I sniffed dismissively, and turned to my child. 'I *am* going to be a *great mother*,' I said. 'Well, I'm going to do my best. Got off to a bit of a shaky start, though.'

'You were in prison!'

'Not what I'm talking about. I mean sodding off on my own right at the beginning of all this. I need to trust other people more; to allow myself to rely on them. None of this would have happened...' I drifted off into thought. Claire reached over and squeezed my hand.

Again, we sat in silence for a few moments. Then Sophia said, slightly nervously: 'Query... have you decided on a name for your son?'

I looked down at the still, golden head, and then up at Sophia's eager, worried face.

'Oh yes,' I said, smiling at her. 'And you helped me there, Sophia. It's important, naming a child. And it's all about trust. I am calling him Peter, because he will be my rock.'

It wasn't an ending, after all. It really was a beginning.

* * *

Finally, Joseph received another transmission. Brax was putting things out on a loop and sending them into space, which is a pretty dodgy way of doing things but with all the dampeners or what-have-yous that were flying around at the moment (so Joseph said), it was the only way of hoping I'd get it.

'We hear that the Imperator is dead. I am wondering exactly what you've been getting up to down there. Estimated time of arrival six-oh-eight-two Deirbhile standard.'

We came out of the shed, Claire carrying Peter, Sophia helping me, and stood there gazing at the sky. I took my child back, and held him as Joseph counted down. I checked every few seconds to see if he was still sending out the homing beam. Of course, he was. And then, finally, we saw a black speck in the furthest reaches of the sky. Bigger and bigger it got; from a pinprick to a housefly to a toy space ship to a real space ship – one of Brax's newest acquisitions, a large space yacht. And there it was, lemon yellow and beautiful, coming in on a vertical descent.

The wind whipped my hair back and forth, off my face then over my eyes, then back again. Every time my vision was obscured I was terrified that the yacht would have disappeared by the time I could see again, but of course that never happened. I imagined I could see Brax waving from the cockpit, though that would have been impossible.

I think Claire, Sophia and I must have been feeling the same, because none of us were jumping up and down. We had this feeling that we had to hold our breaths until it had happened, until the yacht was down and we knew it was real. Any movement would be a risk; might dispel the dream. We just stood there, fur, hair and tentacles blowing in the down-draught, none of us speaking. Peter's eyes were wide open, and he was staring up at the yacht too.

Legs came out from the underside of the yacht, and it gradually came to rest. I still couldn't move. But no one shot at it. No armed guards hastened over to it.

A hatch opened in the side, and a ramp thumped out to the ground. A tiny figure stood in the opening for a second, seemingly scanning the surroundings to look for us. I didn't move, but I could actually feel the adrenaline soaring through my system. Finally I took a step forward, then another and another. Claire and Sophia were holding on to my arms, supporting me, but I scarcely noticed. Another figure, bigger than the first, came out of the yacht door. Both started down the ramp.

I could hardly believe I'd once run from these people; now I couldn't run to them fast enough. As we got closer I could see who the figures were; closer still and I could see the apprehension on their faces. I pulled away from Claire and Sophia, and stumbled the last few steps on my own, towards Jason Kane and Adrian Wall. I could hardly drag my eyes from Jason's face: the look of such hurt and apology and fear and amazement that was there, but I had to speak to Adrian first. I held out my arms. 'This is Peter,' I said. 'This is your son.'

Then I got cold feet about giving Peter away, and snatched him back towards me. Claire put a hand on my arm, and I felt her reassurance. I held my child out again. There was awe in Adrian's eyes as he accepted the little bundle. And then I fell into Jason's arms. And I knew that everything must be okay between us, because it was at least five minutes before he mentioned the smell.

I'm going home. I'm going home to the Braxiatel Collection. I have strong arms around me and a baby in my lap, and Ms Jones has sent a picnic basket full of Claire's and my favourite things. And some painkillers. And I'm going to have a bath and read a book, and I'm not going to cause any more deaths today.

Adrian keeps coming over and gazing at Peter. I know he wants to hold him again, but just at the moment Peter is all mine. Claire can take him, or Sophia can take him, but the thing is, they were there; they were part of it. Adrian wasn't.

I'm not being fair, but he'll have to live with that for now. There's a bond that forms between people when they've been through what Claire and Sophia and I have been through, and it's very tough. In all senses of the word.

I remember reading some wise words once – or perhaps they were just an entry on one of those 'motto a day' calendars – something about how true friends can always pick up where they left off, even if they haven't seen each other for years. I think that's probably true. There are some friends who I haven't seen in centuries, but I think we'd get on just as well if I bumped into them tomorrow. Claire and Sophia are going to be friends like that, I'm sure.

And I wonder if something along those lines is why Jason and I seem fated to be together. Only in our case we tend to get on better if we've not seen each other for centuries. It's the seeing each other day to day that takes the effort. But, somehow, I have this feeling that we're going to be making the effort. Oh, I won't count my chickens – must remember to tell Sophia that one – but at the moment, while he's hugging me and making faces at Peter and only occasionally going 'poo' at the whiff, I believe that this time it might actually work. For good.

'He's got your ears,' Jason said to me, looking at Peter critically. 'Adrian's nose, unfortunately.'

'My child has a perfect nose,' I said huffily.

Jason turned to me. 'And I think they must have been overfeeding you in that prison. If you were painted orange, you'd look like a Space Hopper.'

Of course, there was always a chance that it might not work. I carefully chose a large iced bun from the picnic hamper, and proceeded to ignore Jason Kane completely.

After a while, Jason went to start an argument with the robotic pilot who, he felt, wasn't piloting quite as smoothly as he should, and Brax came over to us. There hadn't really been time for reunions or introductions before, he'd wanted to get off Deirbhile as soon as possible, and who could blame him. Sophia was rather excited. 'Good fact: you are Irving Braxiatel of the Braxiatel Collection!' she cried, almost jumping up and down. 'Query: is it true that you have the fabled Oracle of the Lost on your planet?'

Now how did she hear about that one? Not that I know the answer. And Brax was politely enigmatic, drawing her attention on to other 'facts'. I never knew quite how many rare and even unique texts he had in the Collection, and I live there. Amongst other things, he mentioned that he happens to possess the lost diaries of the Roman Emperor Claudius. One of these days I might have a browse and see if the real Agrippina was quite the bruiser her latter-day namesake obviously thought she was. Brax also revealed he has two copies of Issue One of *The Amazing Armadillo Girl*; one of them still with the free Armadillo keyring on the front. I think I may get around to reading that rather sooner. And definitely not nicking the keyring to keep my identity disk on, oh no.

I hadn't let my baby go once since we got aboard the yacht. He didn't seem to mind. He was awake for most of the time, but didn't grumble at all. However eventually, after some prompting from Claire – who, although generally an incredibly sweet, lovely and understanding person, seems to want me to become a saint overnight – I handed Peter over to Adrian. Admittedly I then stood glaring at them both from a distance of mere inches, which is probably why Brax had the yacht's captain carry me bodily out of the room and dump me on a chair in the yacht's lounge. The captain left at a curt nod from Brax.

'He'll be fine,' Brax said, although I wasn't entirely sure which one he was talking about. 'Now, I know you won't want to talk about it' – he's very perceptive – 'but there are some things you need to know. Firstly, the Fifth Axis is finished. Oh, it won't be over for a while yet, but nothing dies the death faster than a failed military organisation. Secondly, forces are already going in to liberate the various Axis prisons and prison camps all over the galaxy. No innocent person will be incarcerated insofar as anyone can be certain of such a thing. And lastly…' – he gave me a very grave look – 'you have a wonderful child. And I'm sure you are going to be a wonderful mother.'

I gazed up at him. 'People died,' I said. 'A lot of people died.'

'People die,' he replied sadly, and left. I'm not entirely sure what he meant. I don't think he was just being philosophical. But I don't know if he was aiming at comfort or censure.

19
Being a Great Mother

I spent the next few weeks in bed, with the curtains drawn. I've had transfusions and operations and scar reduction treatment, all topped off with an extremely large dose of bright pink antibiotics. Everyone has been waiting on me hand and foot, which is not normally my thing but I rather appreciated it just then. Ice cream and milkshakes were available twenty-four hours a day, in *any flavour I liked*. The planetoid branch of Starbucks even set up a home delivery service for me. People talk about the difficulty of regaining their figure after pregnancy. This is the reason why. Mister Crofton brought me bunches of his prized chrysanths, and even Ms Jones was seen to put her head round the door, pretending that some foolish delivery boy had mistakenly brought an extra doughnut/trashy crime novel/pair of fluffy slippers, and so she'd brought them to me to stop them going to waste. Claire was helping Adrian to look after Peter, although he spent a lot of time in the cot beside my bed. He's never made a sound since... since that time, though. Not when any of us were listening, anyway. I'm not able to feed him because of the various drugs and so on – and because I wasn't well nourished enough anyway, Claire says – which was a sort disappointment to me, but he takes his bottle happily enough. Sophia had gone off, but had promised to visit soon. Brax was being his usual understanding self. And Jason... well, Jason wasn't visiting dive bars or bringing back women and spilling all our secrets anymore. It's going to be a long road before... well, I don't know what, really. But we'll make it.

It all sounds sickly sweet, doesn't it? Happy ever after, too good to be true?

It can't ever be fully happy ever after, because I'm haunted by too many things. But right now I want sickly sweet. I want the love and the hugs and the fairy-tale ending. So you're just going to have to grin and bear it. Oh, and by the way, there's worse to come. Those of a cynical disposition may want to leave now.

Of course, not everything went smoothly. Jason was the first one to bring up the subject. I suppose I shouldn't really have been surprised. 'I know you're calling it Peter,' he said.

'*Him* Peter,' I corrected. 'I'm calling *him* Peter.'

'Um… after me?' he said.

I stared at him. I had actually quite forgotten his middle name was Peter, despite having spent a brief time yelling 'Jason Peter Kane-Summerfield!' whenever he forgot to put the toilet seat down or one of those many other irritating things that husbands do. 'No,' I said, eventually. 'He's his own person.'

He persisted. 'But the names go so well together… Jason Peter… Peter Jason…'

I just laughed. 'Why don't you go and have a sandwich, Jason *Peter* Kane, and leave me to do the thinking.'

He humphed a bit at that. But still went to get a sandwich.

Adrian was next.

'A Killoran child should proudly bear a warrior's name!' he told me. 'Adrian is such a name!'

'Yes, it is,' I agreed, once again wondering why I could never bring myself to tell him that 'Adrian Wall' hadn't been the great Earth leader he assumed. 'But "Peter" is also a warrior's name. There was a ruler on Earth called "Peter the Great". So called because he was, um, great.'

'But Adrian –'

'– is a lovely name, but it's your name. We don't want to confuse the little chap, do we? Now, haven't you got some grouting to do?'

He went with a bad grace. I'm glad I don't understand Killoran. Some of those growls didn't sound at all friendly.

* * *

I was half-expecting to get a note from Avril (she doesn't come up to the surface if she can help it), demanding I name him Peter Avrilus or something equally absurd, but actually the next person to bring up the topic was Brax.

'I believe it is a custom of Earth,' he told me, 'to give a child a name to which he can aspire. Your friend Sophia was telling me as much on the journey home. To name him, for example, for someone who he is raised to think of as a guide, as a source of wisdom, as a –'

'Prat?' I finished for him. (Although somehow I doubted that was what he was going to say. Sometimes I can be very perceptive.)

Brax sniffed at me.

'Hey!' I said, opening my eyes in an expression of girlish amazement, 'I've just thought of something! Inadvertently, Brax old friend, you may have just given me an idea!'

Unbelievably, he actually bought it. I could see him mentally preening himself.

'I could call my baby... Peter *Irving* Summerfield!'

Now he was purring as loud as the Wolsey who'd got the cream.

'Although,' I said, affecting a slight frown, 'He should really have a feminine influence too. A name for his mother.'

Brax nodded, looking understanding.

'So perhaps I should give him my middle name as well. He can be Peter Irving Surprise Summerfield.'

'What an excellent, excellent idea –' Brax was saying when I cut him off.

'Then you can be the one to embroider his initials on all his school stuff, *Irving*,' I told him.

It took him a couple of seconds, but then, to give him his due, he laughed.

'Better luck next time,' I told him as he left the room. And then sat there thinking to myself, next time? What the hell am I talking about? Once is quite enough, thank you very much.

I had actually thought of the middle name I was going to

give my son, but I wasn't going to explain it to anyone else – Jason least of all. You don't rub your hubby's nose in your lost loves, even if he is your *ex*-husband, and even if the nose-rubbing image is actually quite disgusting now I come to think about it. I knew a very noble man once, and I loved him, and he died. Adrian and Brax should be pleased if I ever did deign to tell them the story behind it – I would be giving him a warrior's name, and the name of someone who I would want him to look up to. But I don't think I'm likely to tell them about it – some things are best left in the past. That I like the name should be quite enough explanation for anyone.

The naming ceremony took place on a chilly November day. Peter was wrapped up warm in a blanket that Claire had weaved from her own fur. I know that sounds a bit gross, but it's a Pakhar tradition and rather sweet when you think about it. I had insisted that the naming would take place outside, though. I wanted the Goddess to be able to look straight down on him. If she's up there. And, who knows, maybe my mum's up there too.

We had gathered up as many as possible of the people I wanted to be important to my baby. There'd been a few tears in the planning. One day, incredibly, I had got up and found my own father sitting in the hall of mirrors, having croissants with Brax. My father had been living on twentieth-century Earth last thing I knew, and I certainly hadn't put his name on the list, so this was a bit of a surprise.

My father and I are on interesting terms. We lead separate lives (the centuries that divide us having seen to that), and I don't think we will ever be father-daughter close. But then, we still don't really know each other. 'Ancestors are important,' Brax said to me. 'The generations should be represented as a child is introduced to the world.'

He shouldn't have said that. Because it made me think.

'When I've thought of my father, I've thought of him as alive,' I told Brax, 'because last time I saw him he was. And

I knew I could probably visit him, if Jason and I got our act together time-ring wise. But I know that really, he isn't alive. He was living in the twentieth century, and now it's almost the twenty-seventh. He'd be long dead.'

Brax nodded at me. 'Seeing things in five dimensions... it can be confusing.'

'But you've brought him here. Even though, now, he's dead.'

I could see he didn't know where this was going. It all came out in a rush. 'So you could get my mum too. Bring her here while she's still alive. Let me see her again. Let her grandson know her.'

He put out a hand to me. 'Oh Benny...' he said. 'It doesn't work like that...'

But I couldn't stop. I was balling my eyes out. 'I loved my mother so much...'

'Which is why you couldn't ever lose her again. It would be too cruel.'

'Grief is the price we pay for love!' I cried.

He grabbed my shoulders. 'And you've already paid! You can't go on paying and paying. The price is too high for anyone to bear. You must not lose your mother again.'

And then I came out with something that was a bolt from the blue. I really didn't know up till then that it had been in my mind. 'What if my baby loses his mother too? How I can I ever go anywhere, do anything, risk anything again? I can't condemn him to that!'

I think Brax may have been crying a bit too by that point, but my eyes were too misty to make it out. I only got the idea by the way he cleared his throat before speaking. 'You will do whatever it takes to make this baby grow into a wise and good man, Benny,' he told me. 'You will condemn him to unhappiness only if you refuse to be yourself. Bernice Summerfield is the mother of this child, and so the mother of this child must be Bernice Summerfield.'

I really howled then. But it was sort of good howling.

* * *

The naming was to take place beneath a canopy of trees by the lake, the winter air warmed by a roaring pyre. I wanted Peter to be close to the five spiritual elements: wood, water, air, fire and metal. For the latter he would wear a naming band, a delicate thing made from a silvery metal I couldn't identify. I'd found it on the pillow next to me one morning when I woke up, with a note that read: 'he will be worthy of you'. I had a very good guess as to who had left it there. Typical of him not to hang around to say hello. I suppose he didn't want to complicate my life even further.

I'd introduced my best friend Keri to my other best friend Claire, and the two of them were rubbing whiskers like nobody's business. Relationships syllogisms don't usually work, but this time I think is an exception: she is my best friend, she is also my best friend, therefore they are going to be best friends with each other. 'Yeah?' I asked Keri. 'Could be, yeah,' she replied.

Sophia had arrived the day before, and acted like she'd gone to Slawcor. In recognition of her immense bravery, Brax had granted her *unrestricted access* to the entire Collection. I mean, even I don't have that! It was a job and a half to drag her away to come to the ceremony, I can tell you. But as the person who had given me the name in the first place, she had to be there. While I was showing her to the archives – and trotting to keep up with her eager pace – I suddenly thought of something. 'All that time we talked about names, and you never told me what "Bernice" means,' I said to her.

Her facial tentacles wobbled in a way I recognised as being akin to a Grel smile. '"Bernice"?' she said. 'Good fact: the name Bernice means "Bringer of Victory".'

'Oh,' I said, slightly bashful. 'That's nice.'

'It *is* a good fact,' she flubbered.

I tell you, by the time we reached the archives I was blushing hugely.

There had been something more I'd talked about with Claire

and Sophia earlier.

'I'd like you to be his godmothers,' I said, but shushed their cries of 'Oh, Benny!' and 'Good fact! Good fact!' I had a bit of a speech to get out.

'"Godmother" may not be the most accurate term, but "Goddessmother" is too much of a mouthful, and anyway, it's tradition,' I said. 'But it's not going to be an easy ride, so I want you to think about it before you agree. You were both responsible for saving his life, and that of his mother. You showed yourselves to be unbelievably brave and selfless, and, what is more, to be true friends and good people. I love my child. But… I still don't know if he's mine – no, don't say anything!' Claire had been going to protest. 'And even if he is mine, that doesn't mean he will grow up to be a good person, even though I will do everything in my power to make that the case. Which is why I want there to be good people who will be there for him. If he has choices to make, I want there to be people who will always point him towards the good path. He might still make the wrong choice – what we think of as the wrong choice – but if he takes the dark path it won't be through lack of guidance.'

There were more tears at that point. Honestly, this hormone thing must be catching.

There were other friends from my past who'd made the trip: my former students Michael Doran and Jayne Waspo (not, I hasten to add, as a couple), now all grown up. Emil, Tameka and her now quite large son Scott (Tameka had settled into motherhood so well – I only hoped I would look that radiant still, in a few years' time). I saw Chris (at least I think it was Chris, he looked rather older than the kid I'd last seen, but the unexpected was only to be expected, apparently) and hovering nervously waving now and again were Arko, Forno and Shell. And then there was Starl, sensibly keeping out of both Adrian's and Jason's ways, as if he knew who they were without being introduced. I was going to have a lot of catching up to do later on. Plus there were a lot of Killorans, whose names I was trying very hard to remember. Avril hadn't turned up, thank goodness – that would have taken a bit of explaining to the father's family.

Jason wandered over at one point, shaking his head. 'I don't know *any* of these people,' he moaned. 'It's just like our wedding.' And then he smiled, and shot me a look that almost frizzled my heart. 'And do you remember what we did after our wedding?'

'Yes,' I replied with a smile, 'we shouted at each other for several months and then got divorced.' But we didn't break eye contact. I think this may mean he has finally come to terms with the situation. Thank goodness.

It was time for the ceremony. The service, to be taken by Brax, was very simple. We took Peter round to all the guests and introduced him to them, and then Brax would present him to the universe. Sounds a bit pretentious, written down like that (in fact Jason had stuck a finger down his throat and made gagging noises when we'd talked about it earlier. He has no soul), but I knew it would be beautiful.

I had to walk into the centre of the circle of guests, between the wood and the water, and hand Peter to Brax.

I had to do that right now.

I was standing on the outskirts of the circle. Brax was in the middle, Claire and Sophia just behind him. Adrian was nearby, looking proud and expectant.

Brax raised an eyebrow at me, to let me know the time had come.

And I couldn't do it.

I couldn't walk in front of all those people, into the open, where they would all be *watching me*. I thought back to that poor woman in the prison, the one who'd been clinging to the walls before they dragged her away. She hadn't been able to move, and I suddenly knew how she felt. Waves of vertigo crashed over me, and I thought I was going to fall. Slowly, eyes were turning to look at me, wondering why I wasn't moving. Friendly eyes; Claire's and Jason's and

Doran's and my dad's, but each gaze stabbed my heart with panic.

They were all watching me.

I took a step back. And another. I managed to turn, and I stumbled away. There were cries coming from the crowd behind, but I couldn't make out what they were saying over the roar of panic in my ears.

Claire found Peter and I inside my wardrobe. Joseph told her where I was, the little electronic sneak. It had seemed a good place at the time. Nothing can see you if you're inside a wardrobe, unless of course it's one of those magical varieties where nosy fauns and beavers and lampposts and whatever are hanging around to stare at you. And mine wasn't, because I'd vetted it very carefully and anyway I don't think you get magical plasti-wood. Wardrobes are actually quite comfortable places to be, because you can make a big pile of jumpers to sit on. And, have I mentioned? No one can see inside.

'Everyone was looking at me,' I told her.

'I know,' she said.

'You and Sophia aren't being this pathetic,' I said.

She smiled. 'Sophia and I aren't on display today.'

'I suppose you're going to tell me to get right back on the horse,' I said to her. 'To go back in front of that circle, because they're all people who love me and care about me and understand, and if I don't do it now I might stay shut in a wardrobe for ever?'

'No,' she said, 'I was going to ask if you were comfortable enough, or if you wanted me to fetch some more jumpers. But now you mention it...'

Claire reached out and took Peter from me, leaving me to get up. It was difficult, and I don't mean just because of my still-overlarge waist size.

When we got back to the lake, I found that the circle had spread out. It was more informal now. Little groups were clustered together, talking, and some people had sat down on the grass. Brax seemed to be having a lively discussion with Sophia. As I walked over, the eyes began to turn to me again. I felt terrified. So utterly, utterly exposed. Some people looked hurriedly away, obviously realising, and the sense of relief as each gaze left me was incredible. But I had to keep doing this. And then suddenly the people were getting up off the ground, and the little groups of people were headed towards me, and for a desperate moment I prayed for the earth to open up beneath me. But I found myself surrounded by people. People by my side, people talking to me, pulling at my arms, stroking Peter's head. Suddenly they weren't all staring at me, they were all *with* me. I can't quite explain, but I wasn't exposed any more, I was part of them. And so when they had delivered me to Brax and faded back into a circle, leaving Peter and I in the middle, I didn't feel that I was being stared at, observed; I felt that I was still part of this group of friends, just a part that happened to be standing slightly apart from the rest of the group, and their friendly eyes just happened, naturally enough, to be looking in my direction, wanting to be part of this experience, wanting to give me strength and courage.

Had I been drinking the champagne, I would probably have told them all that I loved them by now.

I took Peter round to everyone. Claire had shot me a 'shall I come with you?' look, but I shook my head and said I'd do it alone. I'd manage. People cooed over him, which was only natural because he is obviously the best baby the world has ever seen. Then, when we'd done our circuit, Brax took Peter and handed him first to Claire, then to Sophia, then held him up high and announced: 'This is Peter Guy Summerfield.' Then he handed him back to me.

I whispered my own version of the ritual into the tiny ear. 'Universe, this is Peter Guy Summerfield. Peter Guy Summerfield, this is the universe. And we're going to enjoy it together.' The ceremony was over.

Adrian had suggested fireworks, but I thought that might

be a bit much for a baby to take, even if, yes, he was born to a proud warrior tradition or, as Jason put it when he heard, being my son he should be able to handle big bangs.

There were champagne cocktails in crystal flutes, but as part of being a good mother, I only had one. Admittedly, however, I had that one topped up a few times.

I crept away while the party was still going. Jason and my dad were renewing their acquaintance over by the buffet table; which basically means they were arguing. In between cheese-and-pineapple on sticks and veggie sausage rolls, that is.

I had a visit to make. I walked around to the recently-built coffee shop, Peter slumbering in the sling across my chest. A uniformed shop assistant called out 'double mocha extra whipped cream and sprinkles?' as I passed by, but I waved a polite 'not today thank you' and carried on. Round the back, just next to the recycling bins (did you know that coffee grounds make great fertiliser? No? Until recently, neither did I. Mister Crofton says they're a very good source of nitrogen. See, isn't this educational?), there is a hole which leads to a tunnel, which leads to a hideaway deep inside the planetoid, which is the home of Avril Fenman, the 'Crystal Sorceress'. These days, I can more fully understand the desire to live in a hole in the ground. Avril is, as I explained earlier, many hundreds of years old, but she looks like a fairly chunky man in his forties. She has a bushy moustache. When I delved into the candle-lit gloom, I discovered that today she was wearing a pink sequined ballgown. Apparently, because she missed out on a lot of fashions while she was incorporeal, now she intends to catch up, whether they suit her or not. She stared up at me, but said nothing.

I held out Peter, but then changed my mind and hugged him to me again. 'This is Peter,' I said. 'He's mine.'

She raised an eyebrow, but still didn't speak. 'He is!' I insisted. 'He has my ears!'

I'm not sure what I was hoping for. Some

acknowledgement that he's mine, all mine, something to silence those still-present nagging doubts. I mean, it's not that I don't love him. I think it's fairly clear by now that I do. And you can't see someone pulled out of your stomach and not feel some deep attachment to them (unless you're in the film *Alien*). But still... oh, as I'd explained to his godmothers, I'd love him whatever, it's just...

Well, there's nature versus nurture (I haven't yet decided on where I stand) and the fact that one of his potential mothers is an evil cow (not me), and that I'd wanted my child to be a fusion of me and Jason, but if not then just to be part of me and I was resenting Adrian having a gene-share and anyway, I know Peter will be his own person but, but, but...

Avril still being silent, I turned to leave.

Her deep voice came after me, as I climbed the tunnel. 'You say he's yours. So he is yours. But you'll always be watching him. Waiting, just in case, one day, heredity strikes.'

I told you she was an evil cow.

Peter was by now fast asleep in my arms, and I wanted to put him to bed. I lay him in his crib, the pakhar fur blanket over him, and then just sat and watched him for a while. I felt utterly content. Nothing could worry me ever again. I had given my legacy to the world, and he was beautiful.

After a while, I left him, and went into my study. There was something I wanted to find, and I thought it was in one of my desk drawers.

Half and hour later I had to conclude that it wasn't. And half an hour after that I concluded that it wasn't in my wardrobe either, or the chest of drawers by my bed, or inside any of a dozen shoe boxes. Eventually, it turned out to be in a biscuit tin. Wonderfully, there was also a chocolate biscuit in there, which I ate.

'It' was an engraved necklace. I studied the words written on it carefully for a while, and then went and sat at my desk.

On a piece of paper, I wrote the following words:

Peter Summerfield is the child of a human being, and I know that he will be capable of being cruel and cowardly. But, though he may get caught up in violent events, his mother will teach him to be a man of peace.

I folded the paper, and went to put it under my baby's pillow.

Acknowledgements

Thanks go to Justin Richards, Paul Cornell and Gary Russell for allowing me to borrow their various creations; to Simon Axon for teaching Joseph about harmonics, and to my wonderful mum for answering all my questions about having a baby. Any mistakes are, of course, down to me and not to them.

About the Author

In her last Bernice book, Jacqueline Rayner wrote about being a man. In this one, she's written about giving birth. At some point she plans to write about something of which she actually has some experience herself.

Also Available

PROFESSOR BERNICE SUMMERFIELD AND THE DEAD MEN DIARIES

A short story collection edited by
PAUL CORNELL

ISBN 1–903654–00–9

Who but Professor Bernice Summerfield, interstellar archaeologist, raconteur, boozer and wit, would get other people to write her autobiography – albeit under threat of death from two bounty hunters sent by a publisher far too concerned about little things like deadlines?

These stories are an ideal introduction to the life of Bernice Summerfield: falling off cliffs, getting sacrificed to orange pygmies, saving the universe and trying to buy a new frock.

Cliffhanging escapes! Adventure on distant planets!
Scones for tea!

The anthology includes new stories by SF author Kate Orman, *Queer as Folk* script-editor Matt Jones and Steven Moffat, the creator of *Coupling*, alongside Mark Michalowski, Daniel O'Mahony, Eddie Robson, Cavan Scott & Mark Wright, Dave Stone, Kathryn Sullivan and Caroline Symcox.

Also Available

PROFESSOR BERNICE SUMMERFIELD AND THE DOOMSDAY MANUSCRIPT
A novel by
JUSTIN RICHRDS

ISBN 1–903654–04–1

The Doomsday Manuscript is the key to finding the Lost Tomb of Rablev and, legend has it, if the tomb is ever opened, the world will end. With the party at the Braxiatel Collection (home to one half of the Doomsday Manuscript) to celebrate the new millennium underway, Benny finds herself drawn into a web of mystery and intrigue that starts with death and gets more serious at every stage. Can she find the second half of the Doomsday Manuscript before it falls into the wrong hands?

Then there's the Fifth Axis, a callous force which assimilates territories and acquires art treasures and other archaeological finds, who are very interested in Kasagrad – the last neutral planet in the Assimilated Territories. Strategically vital and protected from the Fifth Axis by its impenetrable defence systems, will Benny find the Lost Tomb there? And can she squeeze in another drink at "Piccolini's" – favourite haunt of black marketeers, spies, counterfeiters, Fifth Axis officers, and desperate archaeologists – before the end of the world?

Also Available

PROFESSOR BERNICE SUMMERFIELD AND THE GODS OF THE UNDERWORLD
A novel by
STEPHEN COLE

ISBN 1–903654–23–8

There's a whisper going round that the long-lost temple of the Argian Gods of the Underworld has finally been discovered on the planet Venedel. There's an even quieter whisper that deep inside it lies the Argian Oracle, an ancient artefact that can pinpoint the whereabouts of any soul in the universe. Benny Summerfield sets out to see if this is true – perhaps it can tell her the whereabouts of her missing ex-husband, Jason Kane.

Venedel, however, is under siege from an over-zealous Federation, starving the planet until the people capitulate to its terms. Despite this, a team of Nishtubi mercenaries are running the blockade to supply aid for the Venedelans. But why? They have nothing to gain.

Caught between jingoistic natives, Nishtubi heavies, a plague of ancient killers and the secrets of the Gods of the Underworld, Benny faces a great deal of trouble – and has nowhere to run…

Also Available

PROFESSOR BERNICE SUMMERFIELD AND THE SQUIRE'S CRYSTAL
A novel by
JACQUELINE RAYNER

ISBN 1–903654–13–0

Legend tells of an evil sorceress who used the power of
magical crystals to transfer her mind into the bodies of others.
Her reign of terror was long and bloody, and her final defeat
the cause of great rejoicing.

But that's just a legend. A story told to children. Isn't it?
I mean, it's ridiculous. It couldn't have really happened…
could it?

Finding the last resting place of the Crystal Sorceress is an
archaeological dream on a par with discovering the Holy Grail.
So it's hardly likely that someone will just offer the solution to
Professor Bernice Summerfield on a plate.

But sometimes the unlikely actually happens. And one thing
that's very, very unlikely is that Benny will suddenly find herself
to be a member of the opposite gender…

Also Available

PROFESSOR BERNICE SUMMERFIELD AND THE INFERNAL NEXUS

A novel by
DAVE STONE

ISBN 1–903654–16–5

Acting on an abstruse tip-off from the renowned paraphysiologist Dr Rupert Gilhooly (a man who, like, knows a lot of stuff) one Bernice Summerfield has found herself on a probe-ship heading deep into the Problematic Heart of the galaxy – not knowing what, or quite who, she might find.

What she finds is Station Control. A place that exists, simultaneously, in four hundred and seventeen dimensions, a brawling, souk-like Nexus between every world that can, or has or ever will be. And one of those dimensions is Hell.

Bernice knows nothing of the rivalries and power-plays going on here. So she blunders right into them and makes a complete hash of everything, natch.

And one of the particular whoms she finds, quite frankly, what with one thing and another, she could quite well do without. In her current state.

Also Available

THE AUDIO DRAMA ADAPTATIONS

starring Lisa Bowerman as Benny

Big Finish Productions is proud to present the Bernice Summerfield audio adventures, based on novels published originally by Virgin Books!

Featuring all-new music and sound-effects, these full-cast plays are available on CD from all good specialist stores, or via mail order from
www.bernicesummerfield.com

1.1 *Oh No It Isn't!*
adapted by Jacqueline Rayner from the novel by Paul Cornell

1.2 *Beyond the Sun*
adapted by Matt Jones from his own novel

1.3 *Walking to Babylon*
adapted by Jacqueline Rayner from the novel by Kate Orman

1.4 *Birthright*
adapted by Jacqueline Rayner from the novel by Nigel Robinson

1.5 *Just War*
adapted by Jacqueline Rayner from the novel by Lance Parkin

1.6 *Dragons' Wrath*
adapted by Jacqueline Rayner from the novel by Justin Richards

Also Available

THE BRAND NEW
AUDIO DRAMA SERIES

starring Lisa Bowerman as Benny

Big Finish Productions is proud to present on-going fully-original
Bernice Summerfield adventures on single CDs!

Featuring all-new music and sound-effects, these full-cast plays
are available from all good specialist stores, or via mail order.

**2.1 *Professor Bernice Summerfield
and the Secret of Cassandra***
by David Bailey

**2.2 *Professor Bernice Summerfield
and the Stone's Lament***
by Mike Tucker

**2.3 *Professor Bernice Summerfield
and the Extinction Event***
by Lance Parkin

**2.4 *Professor Bernice Summerfield
and the Skymines of Karthos***
by David Bailey

If you wish to order any of our books or CDs, please contact
PO Box 1127, Maidenhead, Berkshire. SL6 3LN.
Big Finish Hotline 01628 828283.

For more details visit our website
www.bernicesummerfield.com

Coming Soon

THE BRAND NEW AUDIO DRAMA SERIES CONTINUES INTO 2002

starring Lisa Bowerman as Benny

Big Finish Productions will release a third season of original audio adventures on CD during the new year, starting in February with

**3.1 *Professor Bernice Summerfield
and the Greatest Shop in the Galaxy***
by Paul Ebbs

and continuing in April with

**3.2 *Professor Bernice Summerfield
and the Green-Eyes Monsters***
by Dave Stone

Plus, in July,
***Professor Bernice Summerfield
and the Plague Herds of Excelis***
by Stephen Cole

Also, in September, to celebrate Benny's tenth anniversary, she returns to the printed word in a deluxe hardcover anthology book, edited by her creator, Paul Cornell, entitled
A Life of Surprises

For more details visit our website
www.bernicesummerfield.com